"Everyone is wondering who you are."

Blake took her hand in his. He ran his thumb over her skin as their fingers laced together.

"Well, why should I be the only one who wonders that?" Amaris teased him with a smile. "I used to know who I was, but these last few days have turned my world upside down. Does that make sense?"

"It does to me. I feel the same way. You put sunshine in my life."

Amaris glanced over her shoulder at the group of richly dressed people. "You weren't exactly living a cheerless existence before I came along."

"No, but it seems that way in retrospect. I didn't realize how much I was missing until I met you." He cupped her cheek in the palm of his hand. "I can't imagine a life without you."

ABOUT THE AUTHOR

To fans of romance fiction, Dan and Lynda Trent need no introduction. Coauthors of over thirty books, including books for Harlequin Superromance, Harlequin Historicals and Harlequin Temptation, this husband-wife team continues to craft award-winning fiction in both the historical and contemporary genres.

Follow Your Heart is a story of romance between two people from vastly different socioeconomic backgrounds, told not only from the perspective of our five senses, but from a sixth, as well. A broad range of subjects remain just beyond the boundary of man's knowledge, but they've become commonplace for the heroine, while most of those around her remain skeptical.

Dan and Lynda enjoy hearing from their readers and will answer all letters personally. Please write them at the following address:

Dan and Lynda Trent
P.O. Box 1782
Henderson, TX 75653

LYNDA TRENT

FOLLOW YOUR HEART

Harlequin Books

TORONTO • NEW YORK • LONDON
AMSTERDAM • PARIS • SYDNEY • HAMBURG
STOCKHOLM • ATHENS • TOKYO • MILAN

Published February 1992

ISBN 0-373-16427-0

FOLLOW YOUR HEART

Chapter One

Amaris Channing was suddenly aware of a sense of impending doom as she made her way down the winding mountain road toward Chinquapin. The fine hairs on the nape of her neck stood erect and she felt a tingling sensation race across her shoulders and down her arms to her fingertips, as though she'd suffered a mild electrical shock. She tightened her grip on the steering wheel and brought her full attention back to the road and the sharp curves that she'd traveled so often that the drive had become routine. Gingerly she tested the brakes. The pedal was firm and the car slowed as it should. She tested the steering wheel, first left, then right, and concluded that her car was not the problem.

But Amaris didn't dismiss the physical sensation as a random twinge of her muscles, as some might have, for she knew from years of experience to pay attention to such subtle signs. Often, her intuition proved to be more reliable than her logic and reasoning. As she stilled her mind, it came to her that *she* was not the one in danger. She stole a glance across the Appalachian Mountains, still misty in the pearl-gray light of dawn as if the answer were out there somewhere. At once she was certain the message had come from her friend Grace. By now, Grace would be at the café waiting for her. And she was in trouble. Amaris pushed down on the accelerator and focused her attention on getting to the café as quickly as possible, chastising herself all the while for choosing this particular morning to go up the mountain to the special place she often visited to greet the dawn, instead of driving directly to work.

Ten minutes later, she slowed as she approached the Mountain View Café. Out front was a lone car, which she didn't recognize. As she drove into the parking lot, she peered through the windows of the log-cabin structure into the dining room, hoping for a glimpse of Grace. There she was, standing near the cash register, talking to a man whose back was to the window. Amaris jerked to a stop and watched the pair for a minute, trying to determine if the man was causing trouble.

Since receiving the danger message from Grace, Amaris had been trying to tune in to her to see what the problem was, but all she could pick up was a red haze, which, from Grace, could be either fear or anger. Now that she could see her, she knew it was a bit of both. Although she couldn't see the man's face, both his hands were in view. He wasn't holding a weapon and didn't appear to be making any threatening moves toward Grace. Concluding that this wasn't a matter for the police, Amaris breathed a sigh of relief and drove around to the back and parked. As she was getting out of her car, the cook arrived, and together they went in through the back door. Whatever trouble Grace was having with the man, she was sure the three of them could handle it.

As Amaris and the cook approached the door to the dining room, the man's words boomed, "Grace, I told you I didn't get myself fired so I'd have an excuse to stop paying child support. That's ridiculous. I was laid off. And why haven't you answered your phone? I've called every evening this week to let you know I wanted to see the boys this weekend. And this *is* my weekend!" Amaris recognized the voice as that of Grace's ex-husband, Lyle Dunlap, and waved the cook aside. Now it was obvious why Grace felt both threatened and angry. She and Lyle hadn't exchanged a polite word since he'd filed for divorce.

As Amaris paused for a moment trying to decide whether to interrupt them or busy herself in the back and let them finish, Grace loudly responded, "I told you not to bother me at work. I've already asked you to leave twice, and if you don't go I'll have to call the police."

"Grace, all I want to know is are you going to have the boys ready for me to pick up at six?"

"Are you going to have the child support you owe me by then?" Grace's voice cracked from her mounting anger, and Amaris could see that this argument was not going to end without intervention. As though she had overheard nothing, Amaris pushed the door open and breezed into the dining room. The couple's conversation abruptly ended. "Grace, I'm here. Sorry I was late. I . . . I'm sorry. I've interrupted you."

"Amaris!" Grace exclaimed, nervously glancing at her watch. "I had no idea it was so late." Then to her ex-husband she stiffly said, "We'll have customers here in just a few minutes. I can't talk now."

Lyle tried to force a smile of greeting to his face as he apologetically turned to Amaris. "I just stopped by for a minute to arrange visitation with my boys. Grace's phone seems to be out of order. I haven't seen you in a while. How have you been?"

"Fine, Lyle. Just fine. If you'll excuse us, we really need to get our table setups done. I know you'll understand." Amaris was uncomfortable being cool toward Lyle, for she felt no animosity toward him, but she had always been much closer to Grace than Lyle and felt she owed Grace the show of support. This was not only a difficult time for Grace, it was a difficult time for them all.

"Yeah. Well, I was about to leave anyway. I'm job-hunting today." To Grace's back as she was walking away, he said, "Six?"

Grace exited the dining room through the swinging door without answering, and anger flushed Lyle's face.

"I don't think she heard you," Amaris offered as an excuse for Grace.

"She heard me, all right. This is my weekend with my boys, but she doesn't want me to have them because I'm out of work. I hate to ask you to do it, but would you try to talk some sense into her?"

"I'll see what I can do." Lyle nodded his thanks, and as he turned to leave, she added, "Good luck with your job-hunting."

Amaris followed him to the door, and after he'd gone she turned around the sign in the window, indicating that the café was open for business, and hurried to the back to get ready.

Grace was sitting at the worktable in the back room, her hands visibly trembling as she struggled to pin her dark blond hair back from her face. As Amaris completed the simple task for her, her heart went out to her friend. With a comforting hand on Grace's shoulder,

Amaris said, "Lyle is gone. Now take a deep breath and let it out slowly. That's it. Everything is okay now."

"I'm so glad you came in when you did. Lyle was getting awfully angry."

"You did pretty well sending your distress signal. I came as quickly as I could, but I'd gone up the mountain this morning. I was relieved to find it was only Lyle."

"Only Lyle?"

"You know what I mean. I see Frank is running a little late this morning, too."

"And it's a good thing. I would have been terribly embarrassed if Frank had seen all that. You know how he is about keeping work and home separated."

"Speaking of home, how are the boys? I haven't seen them in over a week."

A bright smile lit Grace's eyes. "They're both fine. Ben had the sniffles Monday, but his appetite is back now. I don't remember Todd growing this fast when he was seven, but that's been two years. I guess I had forgotten. Ben has already outgrown those tennis shoes I bought him a month ago."

"He's going to be tall."

"He's already almost as tall as Todd." Grace leaned nearer. "I'm afraid Todd has discovered girls."

"At nine? He *is* precocious."

Grace stood with a frown. "That's easy for you to joke about. But the time is coming all too soon when I'll need to talk to him about...well, you know...sex. And I don't know what to say to him." She tucked in a wandering corner of her red plaid shirt and straightened the skirt of her work uniform. "It's not easy raising the children all by yourself."

Amaris stepped closer in commiseration. "I know it must be difficult."

Grace lowered her head and nodded. "When Lyle left us, I thought I would just die, but I kept telling myself I have the boys. Now Todd is growing up and he'll be leaving, too, someday."

"Not for years yet. Give yourself time to get used to the change. The divorce was only final a few months ago. Todd and Ben aren't going anywhere. Knowing those two, I'll bet they both settle down right here in Virginia, maybe even here in Chinquapin, and you'll never really be away from them. Even if they do move away, they'll come home to visit."

With the back of her hand, Grace wiped a tear from her eye. "I know I'm being silly. But it all happened so unexpectedly. I knew we weren't the happiest couple in the world, and I admit we didn't have much in common other than the kids, but I never thought he would leave me. Especially not for someone like Tiffany McNee! She was barely out of high school and didn't even have a job. I never did figure out what he saw in her." Grace snatched her name tag off the board behind the worktable and pinned it on with a stabbing motion.

Amaris wisely said nothing as she, too, pinned her name tag to her plaid blouse and checked to be sure she'd tied her pocket apron straight. She and Grace had been close friends for years, and Grace had always been there when Amaris needed someone to talk to. Returning that gesture in kind was the least she could do.

Grace drew herself up as she checked to be sure she had an order pad in her apron pocket. "I'm sorry to be going on like this. I know you've heard it all before. It's just that this is the second Friday of the month, and you know what that means."

"Visitation?"

"Right. You know, I've been thinking about not letting him see the boys until he gets a job and gets caught up on the child support. I know you're going to tell me I have no right to do that, but I have to do something to make him find work."

"I know you're frustrated, but—"

"That's not the word for it. The boys still have to eat. I still have to buy their clothes and see to it they have the things kids want and need. They can't go without coats just because Lyle can't find a job."

"Lyle did say he was job-hunting today."

"I know. He tells me that every other Friday."

"He's bound to get something soon. I understand Frank's keeping you on through the winter again. Tips won't be quite as good as they were this summer, but your job is secure."

"Thank God for that." Grace went to the linen table and started folding the large napkins in the distinctive manner that was the Mountain View's trademark.

As Amaris joined Grace, she said, "Listen, Grace. If the boys need anything, I'm sure—"

"Oh, no. I couldn't ask you... I mean, it's Lyle's responsibility to provide for the children. Besides, I don't see how you make ends meet without a job all winter."

"I don't have many expenses. I own my house and rarely make long-distance phone calls. My fireplace heats the place quite well, except on the coldest days, and firewood is free for the cutting behind my house. Since I raise most of my own food and eat very little meat, I don't need much money for groceries. Besides, I enjoy having those months of solitude so I can read or write and do my crafts. When the tourists return in the spring, a lot of my handcrafts will sell—especially the baskets."

"I'd go bonkers in a week's time."

"And I don't have two boys to raise, so I can live however I please."

Grace stopped folding napkins and stared at her. "But don't you get lonely out there?"

Amaris paused. "Not too often. When I do, I come visit you and the boys, or one of my cousins here in town. I don't often get lonely." That was true for the most part. But at night when snow lay soft on the ground and the fire crackled in the hearth, Amaris knew there would be times when she would be quite lonely indeed. She was never afraid in her cabin at the edge of town, but she longed more and more for something; no, someone—who? She wasn't sure. At times she felt as if she were teetering on the brink of some great discovery, but she wasn't sure exactly what she yearned for.

The aroma of frying bacon wafted out from the kitchen. As usual, the cook was preparing her own breakfast, a practice Frank encouraged because he not only wanted his cook happy but he wanted the café filled with the inviting smells of breakfast when the first customers arrived. Frank employed the best cooks Chinquapin and the surrounding area had to offer. His menu wasn't elaborate, but it was filled with delicious dishes.

The tinkle of the bell on the front door drew their attention. "There's our first customer, and Frank still isn't here," Grace said. "It's not like him to be so late. Maybe you should call him and see if there's trouble at home. I'll take care of the front." As she started away, she looked back over her shoulder and said, "Thanks for listening. I'll be okay now."

Amaris went to the wall phone and dialed her cousin's number. "Carrie Lou? This is Amaris. Has Frank left yet? Oh? I see. Well, tell him Grace and I have everything here under control and for him not to worry. I'll talk to you later."

She hung up and went back to folding the napkins. Frank was an exacting taskmaster, even over himself. Likely he would blame himself for the fact that his car wouldn't start and might be in a foul mood when he arrived. She hoped, for his sake, she was wrong, but knew that even if he was, as soon as he was assured that his being late hadn't brought on catastrophe, his mood would improve. Frank worried too much, but he was too stubborn for anyone to convince him otherwise. Amaris had always found it curious that Frank trusted his employees to open the café every morning on time, yet felt he had to be there by the time the customers arrived.

Grace came back, her eyes bright with interest. As she shoved the order she'd taken through the kitchen window, she said, "You've got to see what we have in the dining room this morning!"

Amaris was relieved to see the Grace she knew and loved was back. She was always quick to point out the oddball characters. it was like a game. "Oh? It's not another tourist with fifteen cameras and Hawaiian shorts, is it? Seems late in the year for them."

"No, no. He's not like that. Just peek through the door and see for yourself."

"I can't do that," Amaris protested.

"Here." Grace shoved a tray of saltshakers into Amaris's hands. "Pretend you're servicing the counter. Go on out!"

Reluctantly Amaris backed through the swinging door and into the dining room. The decor was rustic, with mountain crafts on the walls and quilts under glass on the tabletops. Live plants were everywhere, and the room was as cozy as bygone days. At a booth on the far side of the room sat a man who looked as out of place in the room as if he had just dropped in from a penthouse in Manhattan. Despite the early hour, he wore a black tuxedo and patent-leather shoes. His tie and collar were loosened, but he still had the air of elegant sophistication. His hair, almost as dark as his formal clothing, was as neatly combed as it must have been the evening before, when he had dressed to go out. Amaris couldn't tell at this distance the color his eyes were, but his skin had a healthy tan as if he were often out-of-doors. The faint stubble of beard on his lean jaw and chin only enhanced his staggering good looks.

As if he sensed her presence, he looked up and their eyes met; Amaris felt the impact all the way to her feet. Neither spoke, and she had to tighten her grip on the tray to keep from dropping it. The cadence of her heart quickened and she experienced the odd sensation of knowing he was a stranger, yet feeling certain she recognized him.

Recognize? Impossible. She had never seen him before. If she had, she would never have forgotten him; she was positive of that. Yet she knew him. She knew him in a way that was as elemental as the mountains.

Trembling from unexpected nervousness, Amaris turned to the counter behind her and began exchanging the saltshakers there with the ones from her tray.

She could feel his unsettling gaze on her back, and her fingers fumbled as she worked. When she could find no other reason to linger in the dining room, she dared glance back at the stranger. He was looking out the window, but she was positive he had been staring at her. Even as she watched, he turned his eyes back to hers.

Amaris clutched the tray, averting her eyes and hurried back to the sanctuary of the back room.

"Well?" Grace demanded. "Have you ever seen anything like that in this restaurant before?"

"Who is he?" Amaris forced herself to say. Her heart was beating so fast she could hardly breathe.

"I don't know. Somebody who had a night out on the town in Roanoke, I guess. We don't get much tuxedo traffic here in Chinquapin, especially not at this time of the morning." Grace put her eye to the crack in the door. "He sure is good-looking."

"Come away from there before he sees you."

"He can't see me through a crack in the door. Not unless he's Superman in disguise."

Amaris was silent. She always knew when someone was watching her, even without having to see them do so. Sometimes she forgot that everyone didn't have such efficient radar.

"Where do you suppose he's from?" Grace whispered as she studied the stranger.

"I've never seen him before."

"Come on," Grace urged. "Read his mind and find out who he is. I'm too nervous to try."

"You know telepathy doesn't work that way. And even if it did, I wouldn't use it just to satisfy my curiosity." She put her face to the crack below Grace's. "He certainly is handsome."

"Yeah," Grace said as she straightened. "Unfortunately, a man who looks as good as he does might not give me a second glance. Shoot, I've never even known a man who owned a tux."

"Maybe he rented it," Amaris suggested, then reconsidered. "No, he looks like the kind who would own it. He looks too at ease in it."

"Obviously he's had it on all night," Grace added. "Must have been an all-night party. Or a very expensive tête-à-tête."

Amaris stepped away and smoothed a loose strand of her hair back from her face. "Wherever he's been or whoever he is, it's no business of ours."

"You're right. Business as usual. I think I'll go see if he wants any more coffee. Or maybe a newspaper."

Amaris nodded. The man was seated in Grace's section, and she was certainly excited at the opportunity to serve him. Even though she knew Grace wouldn't agree to it, Amaris had had the urge to ask her to swap out for this customer. But, then, Grace was the one who was actively looking for a husband.

The bell sounded again, and Amaris stepped out to see three of their regular customers come in and sit at their usual table. With dispatch she greeted them with a smile and a pot of coffee but found herself curiously nervous and distracted as she filled their cups. Was the stranger watching her again? she wondered, but dared not look to find out. She was all too aware of his presence. Never in her life had being in the same room with a man made her nerves strum with such interest. Was he thinking about her? She dared not touch his mind to find out.

Mechanically, she took the order from the men at her table, and smiled in response to their old jokes. After

having to ask one of them to repeat his order, she
forced her attention back to the table she was working
and chided herself for being ridiculous. The stranger
probably wasn't even aware she existed. He most likely
had a wife and kids, or at least a fiancée who claimed
all his affection. As she took the order to the kitchen,
she couldn't resist the temptation to look back at him.
To her chagrin, she found him frankly staring at her
through lowered lids as if he were contemplating her
just as she was him. Amaris blushed and hurried from
the room.

As she busied herself in the kitchen and struggled to
regain her composure, the front door's bell rang twice
in rapid succession. Several of the town's businessmen
had come for breakfast before going to open their own
stores, and they couldn't be kept waiting. Pausing with
her hand on the door to the dining room, Amaris drew
in a deep breath, and for a brief moment she pictured
herself in a spring meadow, surrounded by beautiful
flowers and being soothed by the warmth of a gentle
breeze and the brilliant sun overhead. She had learned
this relaxation technique as a child and over the years
had used it often. Almost instantly she felt steadier.
Why she hadn't thought to do this earlier, she didn't
know. With another calming breath she resolved to
keep her mind on her job, then strode confidently into
the dining room and resumed the routine business of
waiting tables—with the minor exception that she refused to look in the direction of the stranger, a task
which wasn't easy.

On her third trip back to the kitchen, she noticed
Frank hurrying in the back door, a scowl plastered on
his features. Quickly studying his eyes, she concluded
his frown was only superficial. With a bright smile, she

good-naturedly chided him. "It's about time you got here," she said, as she looked at her arm where a watch would have been if she ever wore one. "What if Grace and I came dragging in this late? I'll bet your excuse is car trouble."

"Yeah, the timing was off." He paused for a moment, a smile lurking behind his eyes. "That's right. You called. Thanks for letting me know you two were on top of things here. Looks like we're doing better than usual this morning. I even noticed several cars in the parking lot I didn't recognize. Did you see the black Mercedes out there?"

Amaris hadn't seen the car but instantly connected it with the man in the tuxedo. She shrugged, not wanting to think about the stranger. Frank, however, being much too curious and far less subtle than Grace, pushed open the door and unabashedly looked around. "I'll bet I can guess who drove up in it. Check out the booth by the north window."

Amaris pretended to look where Frank had indicated and nodded her agreement. "I never saw him before," Frank continued as he let the door swing back into place. "Looks like he's coming in from a party. Is Grace taking care of him?"

Amaris tried to answer, but the words seemed to be stuck. After clearing her throat, she said, "Yes, she is."

Frank grinned at her. "Maybe he'll choose one of your tables next time."

She tried to appear nonchalant. "I doubt we'll ever see him in here again. My guess is he's just passing through." All the same, she hoped she was wrong. Even though he'd curiously affected her, she had enjoyed looking at him.

Before long the dining room was filled with the regular crowd, brimming with conversation and laughter, and Amaris was pleased to be able to keep herself occupied and avoided making eye contact again with the stranger. But when Grace announced the man had gone after leaving her a generous tip, Amaris felt a twinge of disappointment that she hadn't been paying attention. Even though it wasn't easy for her to admit it to herself, she had hoped to see him leave so she could satisfy her curiosity as to whether he was indeed as tall as she'd guessed him to be. "I'll clear this table for you. Edna Sanford and her friends just came in and are asking for you."

"I saw them, but they're in your section."

"Edna doesn't pay any attention to little details like that. Go ahead." Amaris grabbed an empty tray and went out to clean the stranger's table.

After she put the dishes on the tray and wiped a damp cloth over the tabletop, she dusted crumbs from the booth seat. A silver gleam from the crease between the seat and back cushions caught her eye. It was a money clip, and as Amaris retrieved it from its hiding place, she saw it contained several crisp bills—the least of which was a twenty. All the others were hundreds. Her eyes widened, and she rushed out the front door to try to catch the man, but he and his Mercedes were gone.

Incredulously she looked back at the money clip and counted the bills. Five hundred and twenty dollars! She looked up the road and tried to will the stranger to come back after his money, but she couldn't reach his mind. Her only other choice was to try to reach him through the money clip, itself. She closed her slender fingers around the cold metal, and as it began to warm

in her palm, pictures formed in her mind. She saw a
house on a hill, against a vista of rolling foothills. The
rose red brick house in her mind's eye was large and
expensive-looking—exactly the sort she could imagine
the man owning—with soaring white columns and an
upper veranda that was as deep as the one below it.
Huge trees and carefully tended gardens flanked the
house, and as she concentrated it came to her that its
name was Eventide.

She drew her brows together and concentrated
harder, trying to get his name. Marshall? That was
similar but not quite right. Maynard? No, Mayfield.
Surety swept through her. His last name was Mayfield. Now for his first name. A jumble of memories of
people she had never seen before and a whirl of places
and events filled her thoughts. At random she selected
one of the faces from the man's memory and stayed
with it for a few moments until she heard him call the
man Blake. Blake Mayfield.

Relief and exhaustion flooded through her, and she
felt drained. In her effort to determine his name and
where he lived, she had scarcely been breathing.
Amaris drew in deep gulps of air. Blake Mayfield of
Eventide. Now all she had to do was find Eventide. She
had a vague feeling it was near Roanoke, but she had
never heard of it.

Suddenly realization hit her. Mayfield? That was the
name of the family that more or less ran the state government. Most of the Mayfields were politicians of one
sort of another. Could he have been one of *those*
Mayfields? Her fingers tightened around the money
clip, and she received confirmation that he was.

She tried to recall anything she might have heard
about Blake Mayfield, but she drew a blank. Politics

held no interest for her, and she knew only that Anthony Mayfield had once been a hopeful in a presidential primary. Was Blake Mayfield the man's son, or perhaps nephew? She couldn't recall any specifics.

"Amaris? What on earth are you doing out here?" Grace asked. "We have a roomful of customers."

"Look. He left his money clip." Amaris showed it to her.

"Look at all that money!" Grace quickly thumbed through it. "There's enough there for you to buy that couch you've been looking at over at Gresham's!"

Amaris's eyes widened in shock. "This isn't my money! The stranger dropped it."

"But you don't know who he is, so you can't return it. That makes it yours, that is if he doesn't come back and claim it within two weeks. That's Frank's policy."

"But I do know his name."

"You told me you weren't going to read his mind."

"I didn't. Not exactly. I got his name through his money clip."

Grace quickly flipped the silver clip over and inspected the other side. "I don't see any name on it."

"No, no. Remember when we talked about picking up on memory traces from objects a person has an attachment to? That's how I did it."

"I've never had any luck doing that. Of course, I haven't tried very often, and you've been doing things like this for years. But that's beside the point. Who is he?"

"I think his name is Blake Mayfield."

"Is he from around here? I don't know any Mayfields. And what a pity."

"I don't know. I got the impression he lives somewhere around Roanoke, but I'm not sure."

"Then how will you return it?"

Amaris put the clip of money in the pocket where she kept her tips. "I'll find a way."

"We'd better get back inside before Frank has to come looking for us. Our customers? Remember?"

Amaris hurried back to work, and although her hands were busy, her thoughts never strayed from the money clip in her pocket.

By closing time she was tired—even more so than usual, because of the mental energy she had expended—but before leaving she stopped to talk to Frank, hoping he could shed some light on her search. "Frank, do you know of a big red house around here called Eventide? It looks like something out of *Gone With the Wind*."

"Eventide? Nope, never heard of it."

"It may not be around the parkway here. Could be over toward Roanoke. I think it's owned by Blake Mayfield."

Frank looked at her as if she were talking nonsense. "*The* Blake Mayfield? The one who's running for governor?"

"Is he? I don't know."

"That's the only one I know of. You know, that man in the tux this morning looked something like him. I didn't think Mayfield was that tall, but you can't tell from television." Frank's face brightened. "Do you think that's who it was? Could be that the next governor of Virginia had breakfast with us this morning. But it probably wasn't him anyway."

"Whether that was him or not, do you know where Blake Mayfield lives?"

"I think you're right about Roanoke. But don't ask me just where. We sure don't run in the same crowd. Why do you want to know?"

"Never mind. I just heard the name and wondered."

Amaris said goodbye and left. All the way home she wondered about the man and how she could return his property to him. She hadn't mentioned finding the money clip to Frank, because she felt a personal obligation to see to it that Blake Mayfield got his money back. Frank would have insisted he hold the money until the man came back to claim it, and if the man didn't remember to check there, it would never get back to him. And she couldn't tell Frank she was sure of the man's name without him pressing her to tell how she knew. Frank was a nice guy, but he was close-minded and superstitious. He'd already overheard her and Grace talking about telepathy and had made it clear that he would brook no such discussions at work. If he were ever to find out she actually could pick up thoughts from other people's minds, he would probably feel too uneasy around her to keep her on, relative or not. No, it was up to her to find Blake Mayfield and give back the money.

On her next day off Amaris showered early, blew her hair dry and set out for Roanoke. The money clip in her skirt pocket felt as if it were generating its own heat. Often when she was ''reading'' an object, it felt unusually hot, and Amaris hoped this meant it would lead her to him.

On the outskirts of Roanoke she stopped at several service stations and a drive-in grocery, inquiring about Blake Mayfield. Everyone she talked to knew of him, but no one could give her directions. Deciding to use

her instincts, Amaris took out the money clip and held
it in her left hand while she drove with her right. After
a short while she found herself on a twisting road that
looked unlikely but felt right. She had expected the
house to be on a main artery into the city, but realized
a more remote location would be better in keeping with
its architectural style. The house likely had been built
long before the modern highway system was designed.

Rounding a bend in the road, her mouth suddenly
went dry and her palms became clammy. Only a few
hundred feet ahead were two massive wrought-iron
gates topped by an archway boldly emblazoned with
the word "Eventide." No one was in sight, and the
gates were open wide. Feeling like a trespasser, Amaris
drove onto the estate.

The road looped over a rise and curved up to the
house she had seen in her mind. Beyond its sculpted
lawn lay the panorama she had seen, only they weren't
mere foothills but mountains. The house's elevation
had misled her. She let the car roll to a stop in front of
the wide white steps, but instead of getting out, she sat,
staring at the imposing structure. Unreasonable apprehension filled her and she asked herself why but got
no clear answer. Neither wealth nor power had ever
intimidated her before, and she had no reason to assume that was happening now. Nevertheless, she was
feeling terribly uneasy. For a moment she closed her
eyes and centered her thoughts on her purpose for being here, then opened her car door, mounted the massive steps and rang the doorbell.

Chapter Two

Blake Mayfield had never been an early riser, always feeling more alive at midnight than at dawn. This Saturday morning had been his first chance in weeks to sleep late, and when Spenser came into his bedroom and awakened him, Blake was not pleased.

"I'm sorry to disturb you, Mr. Mayfield—I thought you were already awake. There's a lady in the morning room who wants to see you."

"A what?" he mumbled groggily. "How did she get in there?"

"I showed her in and asked her to wait." As usual, Spenser showed little emotion and great detachment from the affairs of his employer.

"A lady?" Blake repeated, as he rubbed his eyes and tried to wake up. "Who did you say it is?"

"Her name is Miss Channing. Miss Amaris Channing."

"Do I know her?"

"I have no idea, sir."

Blake sat up and ran his fingers through his thick black hair. "Channing. I don't know anyone by that name. What does she want?"

"She didn't say. Should I go ask?"

Blake picked up his bedside clock and squinted, trying to focus his eyes on its face. "Jeff told me nothing was scheduled today before lunchtime. What could anyone possibly want with me at nine o'clock in the morning?"

"I have no idea. Shall I send her away?"

Blake shook his head. "No, no. I must know her, or she couldn't have gotten past the gate. Channing. I don't know," he said almost to himself. Then, to Spenser, he said, "Give her some coffee and tell her I'll be down in a few minutes. Maybe a shower will wake me up."

Spenser went away, and Blake crossed his thickly carpeted room to his adjoining bath. As he showered he tried to remember where he could have met someone named Channing, who would be able to get past his gate security and show up on his doorstep, unannounced and unexpected.

The past few weeks had been hectic, with a significant increase in the number of political meetings and events his campaign manager, Jeff Hancock, had arranged for him. Blake was tired, but he knew it wasn't the physical demands that had sapped his energy; it was the emotional upheaval of the past several days. First there had been that heated argument with Darla over her insistence that he cancel some of his campaign activities and attend a formal party at her parents' home in Atlanta, so her parents could officially announce their daughter's engagement. She said her parents had been planning the party for weeks, and she was sure she'd mentioned it earlier, but Blake had had no such recollection. Then, there was Darla's demand that they drive to Atlanta rather than fly, because she had suddenly developed a fear of flying.

He had known for weeks that something was wrong between them, but he'd thought the problem was due to the campaign's increasing demands on his time. It was not until an hour before the guests were to arrive that she announced to Blake and her parents that she had changed her mind about marrying Blake. In the privacy of her father's study, Blake talked with her for hours while her parents' guest mingled about, wondering what the special occasion was. Finally, Darla leveled with him. The truth, she said, was that she couldn't marry him because she had fallen in love with someone else. Without another word, he had left for home.

During the long drive, Blake had had a lot of time to think. At first he was angry at her for deceiving him; then he was angry at himself for being deceived. But within hours his anger had subsided, and he was surprised that the great sense of loss he had expected to feel wasn't there. He'd loved Darla and had planned to marry her, yet it was all off now and he felt unexpectedly relieved. The only thought he'd had about this situation that made any sense was the fleeting notion that his love for her must have been based on her profession of love for him. However, he had rejected the idea, because that would have meant he was not in touch with his feelings and that simply wasn't true. Or at least he hoped it wasn't. The only thing he was sure of was that his relationship with Darla Radborne was forever ended and he would have to put all that behind him.

When he'd finally gotten home that next morning and was undressing for bed, he noticed that he'd lost his money clip and over five hundred dollars, somewhere between the Radbornes' house and Eventide.

Although it irritated him that the money was missing,
it was the loss of the money clip that he regretted more.
His father had given him the sterling-silver money clip
the day he graduated from high school, and every day
since he had carried it with him. He had thought about
backtracking to look for it, but he couldn't even remember all the places he'd stopped for gasoline and
coffee and to just walk around so he would remain
alert. And even if he'd remembered and had had the
time to look for it, the odds of it still being where he'd
dropped it were slim.

That morning he had managed to get only three
hours of fitful sleep, when Jeff Hancock called him
wanting to know what had happened between him and
Darla. Jeff said he'd already sidestepped one inquiry
from a wire-service reporter and needed the facts. Reluctantly Blake had invited Jeff to come right on over,
and until the wee hours of the next morning they had
talked about the adverse effects his breakup with Darla
Radborne might have on his bid for the governor's
mansion and planned the strategy they would use to
control the damage. Now there was a strange person
named Channing in his morning room. His private life
seemed to be a thing of the past.

As he shaved, he tried to put a face to the name. She
had to be someone remotely associated with this new
political campaign activity, otherwise he would remember her. Blake had a good memory for names and
faces.

While he dressed in slacks and a burgundy knit
sweater, he thought back to the luncheon in Roanoke
the week before. There had been a heavyset woman
with large teeth and an equally large contribution

promise. What was her name? It must have been Channing.

With the mystery solved, Blake went downstairs ready to thank the matron again for her generous contribution. At the door to the morning room he abruptly stopped. The Channing woman had her back to him, but Blake knew at once she was not the woman with the large teeth. Her shoulder-length hair was Indian straight, as dark as midnight, with bluish highlights. She wasn't tall, but her body was beautifully proportioned. She was wearing a simple federal blue corduroy skirt which swirled softly about her shapely legs, and her tailored oxford shirt was tucked into the waistband of the skirt. About her waist was a plain leather belt. When she turned to greet him, he was struck by her femininity.

For a moment he could only stare. She looked vaguely familiar. He knew he'd seen her before, but he didn't remember where.

"I found your money clip," she said.

Her voice was melodious with a soft southern accent, and as she spoke her lips turned up in a hint of a smile, as if she were more accustomed to smiling than frowning. Her face was heart-shaped; her skin the color of golden ivory. Surprisingly her eyes were clear gray, and they sparkled as if they were lit from within. "What?" he managed to stammer.

"Your money clip. I found it." She opened her hand and held it out to him.

Blake felt as if he were moving underwater, as he took it from her. His eyes never left hers, and when his fingers grazed her warm palm he felt the contact in his soul.

Drawing his gaze away, he looked down at the money clip. Inside the sterling-silver clip was a neat fold of money. Absently he pulled the money free and counted it.

"It's all there."

His eyes returned to her. "Where did you find it?"

"It must have fallen out of your pocket while you were eating breakfast."

"I beg your pardon?"

"At the Mountain View Café in Chinquapin. You had breakfast there the day before yesterday."

Remembrance struck him. "Of course! You were one of the waitresses."

"That's right. I would have brought it back before now, but it took me a while to find you."

"How did you? Find me, I mean? My name isn't on the money clip."

She shrugged and looked away. "I have my ways."

Blake wondered what she meant by that. He had been on television and in the newspapers often lately. That must be it. "I appreciate your honesty in returning this." He peeled off one of the hundreds and held it out toward her. The reward was more than he would ordinarily have offered, but the twenty-dollar bill seemed too little for her trouble. To his surprise, she backed away.

"You don't owe me anything."

"But you drove all the way over here to return it." He frowned in confusion. "How did you get past the guard at the gate?"

"What guard?"

"The guard wasn't on duty?"

"Why do you need a guard to watch over your property?"

Blake studied her curiously. "I have a guard to ensure my privacy."

"It doesn't seem to work very well. I mean, here I am. Anyone could have come in here."

Without looking away from her, Blake called over his shoulder in a loud voice, "Spenser!" When the butler appeared, Blake said. "Check on the guardhouse and find out why the gate was left unattended."

Amaris smiled. "You sound like a general."

Blake held out his hand to her. "We haven't been formally introduced. I'm Blake Mayfield. You're Amelia..."

"Amaris," she corrected. "Amaris Channing."

He extended his hand in greeting and she obliged. Her hand in his was soft and warm. "Amaris is an unusual name."

"Yes, it is."

He realized he was still holding her hand and pulled back self-consciously. "Won't you sit down, Miss Channing? It is 'Miss,' isn't it?"

"Yes, but I can't stay." She moved briskly toward the door.

Blake cast about in his mind for a reason to detain her. She fascinated him more than anyone he had met in a long time. "Don't rush off. Have coffee with me."

"No, thanks. I don't care for coffee."

"Tea, then? Juice or milk?" He found himself wondering what there was about her that seemed so compelling. He was not unaccustomed to meeting beautiful women, nor was she the prettiest he had ever seen, but she was the most intriguing. "You didn't say how you found me," he said, to stall her departure.

She paused. "No, I didn't."

"Then, how..."

"I have to go."

"Spenser." When his butler didn't respond, Blake stepped across the morning room to the doorway and called again, having forgotten he had already sent the man on an errand to the gatehouse. When he turned back, the woman was gone. Hearing the massive front door close, he hurried after her. But by the time he rushed out onto the front porch, she was driving away. "Wait!" he called out, but if she heard him it made no difference.

Thinking quickly, Blake took note of her license-plate number and hurried back into the house to make a call. "Jeff, this is Blake. I want you to trace a license plate and get me an address. Of course, it's important. You can pull some strings, can't you? Thanks."

In half an hour, Jeff called with the name and address. When Blake instructed him to reschedule all his afternoon appointments, Jeff reminded him that he'd already once postponed the luncheon speech he was due to give to the Roanoke chapter of the Daughters of the American Revolution; and he didn't dare put the ladies off again. Jeff was right, and Blake agreed to keep the one o'clock appointment, but he was adamant the two radio interviews and the photo session could wait.

After a meal of cold roast beef and two asparagus spears, Blake pretended to patiently wait for the ladies to make their way through a lengthy business meeting. Then with a broad smile he stepped to the podium and sped through his half-hour speech in fifteen minutes flat. As hastily as he could, he exited the gathering and was on his way to Chinquapin.

AMARIS SAT CURLED in an overstuffed chair in her den, gazing out at the mountain stream that plunged and gurgled just beyond her porch. Although her property extended some three hundred feet past the stream, the rapidly flowing water formed the practical boundary, as the land on the far side rose almost vertically, forming what appeared from her den to be a sheer wall of forested vegetation. The view of the mountain was particularly enjoyable this time of year, as it was awash in a riot of autumn colors. She had acted like a fool to run away from Blake Mayfield that way. Now she would never see him again—not that she would have, anyway. He was a part of the Mayfield political dynasty, and people of such wealth and power kept themselves separated from society as a whole.

Every time she thought about the division between people of different economic conditions, Amaris's emotions became embroiled. Money should have nothing to do with how Blake Mayfield saw her as a person, but she was sure it must. He had offered her a reward for being honest, and a large amount at that, probably because he thought she needed the money. Well, she didn't. Her own pride in her personal integrity was enough to keep her honest. As for everything else, she was probably as intelligent as he was. True, she had had to work her way through college to get her art degree, while he probably had taken a higher education for granted; and she had had to work to learn to speak and dress properly, whereas he had most likely been taught these things from the cradle. But underneath it all, they were just people, human beings. Yet she had run away from him, or rather had chosen to leave before he got the idea that she cared anything at all about getting to know him better. That way there had been no pain or rejection, and that was preferable.

Amaris held up her hands and studied them as if she had never seen them before. It wasn't only economics that set her apart from some people but it was because she was...different. Why did her hands tell her secrets that she shouldn't be able to know? What was it she was supposed to learn from this? What was she supposed to do with the unique ability? Was she different so she would be set apart even from those of her own circle? It certainly had been a challenge to find friends who accepted her, special talents and all. She had Grace and for that she was thankful, but she longed to find a man who was as understanding.

For years her approach to personal relationships with men had been much the same. She would date a man long enough to get to know him well, then she would gingerly introduce him to her special abilities. Once he got to know the real Amaris Channing he would pull away, either because of fear or ignorance of things he didn't understand. Lately she'd decided to be more direct and up-front, hoping the end result would be different.

And even if the esoteric differences weren't there, the social differences were. She supposed it had been silly of her to have so looked forward to seeing Blake Mayfield a second time. Even though she had found him to be more handsome dressed casually, it only whetted her appetite for something she couldn't have. It was best for her to get Blake Mayfield completely out of her mind. She rested her chin in her palm and watched the endless rush of water in the stream.

When a knock sounded on her door, she considered ignoring it. Who else could it be but a salesman? Grace had not mentioned coming over, and she always called first. But then door-to-door salesmen seldom made stops out here because of the distance between houses. The only person it could be was Grace.

When the knock sounded again, Amaris untangled her legs and went to let her friend in. If Grace was in a good mood, that would help Amaris pull herself up out of the blues. If she was down, Amaris's spirits would be lifted as she worked to cheer up Grace. To her profound amazement and dismay, she found Blake Mayfield standing on her porch.

"Good morning," he said as if they were fast friends.

Caught completely off guard, she sharply asked, "How did you know where I live?"

"Have I come at a bad time?"

"Did Frank Anderson give you my address? He knows better than to do that."

"Who is Frank Anderson?" He looked thoroughly confused. "If I'm intruding, I can leave."

"No," she said, quickly gathering her composure and swallowing the lump in her throat. "I mean, come in." She moved aside.

Blake stepped through the doorway and looked around with interest. The house was made of logs, as were many of Chinquapin's buildings, but the color of the wood and the size of the windows indicated it was a fairly new structure. The furniture was covered in blue-and-white chintz and was arranged so that the stone fireplace at one end of the open living space was the room's focal point. At the opposite end, the kitchen, also with blue and white accents, was separated from the main room by a wide counter. A rag rug warmed the floor and tasteful pictures decorated the walls. "I like your house."

"Thank you. If you don't know Frank Anderson, how did you find me?"

"I have my ways," he said with a self-satisfied grin, but when Amaris frowned, he added, "That's all the explanation you gave for finding me. See how confusing that can be?"

"Touché. But I doubt we used the same methods." She motioned for him to sit down, and he did. "Would you like some coffee?"

"I thought you said you don't drink coffee."

"I don't, but I keep it for guests. It's instant."

"That's fine with me."

He watched as she went into the kitchen area and put a kettle of water on the stove top and lit the burner. Who was this Frank Anderson she'd mentioned? A lover?

"He's my boss," she called out.

"What?"

"I said Frank is my boss." Suddenly she stopped and slowly turned to look at him, her eyes filled with apprehension.

"I was wondering who he was, but I never said it aloud."

"Just a lucky guess, I suppose," she said with a nervous gesture. "Do you use cream or sugar?"

"No. No, black is fine."

She could feel his eyes on her, and she was afraid to look at him. Although she had no idea why he had come to see her, she knew that this was not a good time to explain her psychic gifts to him—if, in fact, there ever would be such a time. While pretending to be busy in the kitchen, she collected herself. He was probably here only to insist that she take the reward he had offered her and not for any social reason. When the kettle whistled it was ready, she made his coffee, then poured herself a glass of tap water before going back into the living area.

"I like your house," he said.

"I like yours, too." She smiled at the thought of the vast differences in the two homes. His was palatial compared to hers.

"This place reminds me of a cabin I own in the mountains. I go there on weekends, whenever I can get away."

"I live in mine all year."

"I didn't mean for that to sound the way it must have. I was trying to pay you the compliment of saying your house feels like a home should."

"Oh? How is that?" she asked with growing curiosity. This house was very similar to the one she had lived in with her parents while she was growing up. Most of the houses in town were about the same size and type.

"It feels as if someone really lives here."

Amaris looked at him in surprise. "You can feel that?"

"What to you mean?"

"Never mind."

Blake went over to the window and gazed out at the stream. As Amaris sipped her water, she wondered if he, too, was sensitive to the subtle imprints people left on their surroundings or whether she was trying to read too much into a casual turn of phrase. After a minute she said, "I suppose there are fish out there. I'm no fisherman personally, but—" She stopped as she realized he had turned around and was staring at her.

"You just did it again! You answered a question I didn't ask."

Her mouth felt dry. She had seen that incredulous and wary expression all too often. "I assumed you were wondering that by the way you were looking at the water."

He didn't look convinced. "You're a very observant lady, Miss Channing."

"Thank you," she said faintly. "Call me Amaris."

Blake sat back down and gingerly sipping his steaming coffee. "Why wouldn't you let me repay you for returning the money clip I lost?"

"Because there was no reason for you to do that. The money was yours."

"Most people would have kept it."

"I'm not most people."

He studied her over the rim of his coffee cup. "You're right about that. You aren't quite like anyone I've ever met."

Amaris's eyes flashed indignantly. "I may not run in your social circle, but—"

"That's not what I meant." He replaced the cup on the coaster. It was blazing hot. Blake watched in amazement as she got up, went to the refrigerator, brought back an ice cube and dropped it into his cup.

Silently Blake raised his eyes to hers in an unspoken question. She looked guilty, as if she had again made a mistake. "This goes beyond coincidence," he said at last. "Care to explain?"

"No, thank you."

"Suppose you tell me exactly how you found me and how you happened to approach my gate during the few seconds it took for my guards to change shifts. That was the only time that gate has been left unlocked and unattended in months."

"Coincidence."

He shook his head.

"You won't believe me if I tell you the truth."

"Let me explain. I have guards at the gate to keep people out, and you drove right through. You say you 'found me,' but won't say how."

"I found someone who gave me directions to your house."

"Then, when I was in the restaurant you recognized me from television or the papers? Why didn't you say so? Why all the mystery?"

"I didn't recognize you at all."

"Did the other waitress tell you who I was?"

"No, she didn't recognize you, either."

"Well? Surely you can see how this is making me a bit nervous. In my position, I don't like mysteries."

"I don't mean you any harm. I only wanted to return your money."

"But now you know it's possible to get past my guards."

"Mr. Mayfield, I don't have any interest in getting past your guards or—"

"Call me Blake."

She looked at him in confusion. "Are you upset or not? I can't tell."

"I'm perplexed. You accomplished something the designer of my security system had assured me was impossible."

"Very few things are really impossible. Besides, if you're so worried about security, what are you doing here? Didn't it occur to you I may have led you here to ambush you?"

He smiled broadly and her heart beat faster. "I have to admit that that never occurred to me."

"Good, because I didn't have that in mind at all."

"I still want an explanation," he insisted, serious again. "How did you find me, if you had no idea who I am?"

Amaris drew in a deep breath. She would probably never see him again, and it really wasn't fair for her to have to have made this out to be so mysterious. "I have this . . . gift. I held your money clip in my hand and I concentrated. Once I had the name of your house, your own name came more easily. I had the impression Eventide was in the vicinity of Roanoke. I asked until I found it."

Blake was quiet for several moments. "You expect me to believe that?"

"You can do as you choose, but it's the truth."

"Miss Channing, I think you'd better give me the real explanation. My mind is filling with all sorts of suspicions."

"I thought we were on a first-name basis."

"It depends on your explanation." His hazel eyes were as cool and green as the pine trees beyond the window.

With a sigh, Amaris held out her hand. "Maybe I can show you. It doesn't always work as well as I wish it would, but I'm willing to give you a demonstration, since it is so important to you. Give me something of yours to hold. Anything will do, as long as you know where it came from."

He hesitated, then reached in his pocket and pulled out his keys. He released the ring and handed her the gold key-chain medallion engraved with the initials "M.P."

Amaris neither looked at it nor read the engraving. Instead she closed her fingers about the warm metal and shut her eyes. As soon as she began to concentrate, the images started to form. "This is a key chain given to you by a tall woman with light hair. Her hair is really darker than it appears to be. She bleaches it. She lives south of here. No, she's from south . . . no, wait . . . Georgia, that's it. She grew up in Georgia. Atlanta. Her name is . . ." Amaris paused. Names were always harder to intuit than pictures. "Darling? No, Darla. Darla Radborne. The key chain is something to do with a president."

She opened her eyes and looked at the medallion. "Who is M.P.? Was I wrong?"

Blake was pale and obviously shaken. After a pause he said, "No. You weren't wrong. Her name is Darla Radborne. The part about the president was a private joke that no one knows about except the two of us. M.P. stands for Mr. President. Darla sets her goals rather high."

"She also has more in mind than being First Lady," Amaris retorted. "You aren't the only man she's seeing."

"You're right about that, too. We broke off our engagement this past weekend."

"I should say I'm sorry, but you wouldn't have been happy with her." Amaris touched her fingertips to her lips, as if she hadn't intended to say that. "I am sorry that I said so, however. At times I speak more freely than I really should."

"You are truly amazing," Blake said as if he were weighing each word. "Up until now I never believed in ESP."

"Now you do?"

"Now I'm not sure. I don't know any other explanation for what I just saw. You could have known Darla's name and that she's from Atlanta, but there's no way you could know about M.P. or that she is seeing someone else. That hasn't made the papers yet."

"You don't seem all that upset for someone who just lost a fiancée," she observed, again verbalizing more than she intended and instantly regretting that she'd done so. The amazement on Blake's face was gone.

Blake stood and looked down at her for a long moment. His eyes were troubled and confused. "I'd better be going," he said, but he made no move toward the door.

Amaris got to her feet. "I apologize for upsetting you so much. Next time I'll lie."

He gazed at her. "I have a lot to think about. Is it all right if I call you sometime?"

Amaris could hardly believe her ears. She had told him she was psychic, even demonstrated it for him, and he still wanted to talk further with her.

"Sure. You can find my phone number the same way you found my address. Or you can check in the phone book. I'm the only Amaris Channing in town. My address isn't listed, but I see you already have that."

He grinned and nodded. Mystery went both ways. "I'll call you."

From the mellow tone of his voice, he sounded as if he was interested in her and not just being curious about her psychic gifts. "Or we could make it really simple, and I could invite you back next Thursday. That's my next day off." She held her breath.

"Thursday? I'm not sure I can make it then— I'll have to check with my campaign manager and find out if I'm free."

Realizing how presumptive she'd been and feeling terribly vulnerable, she said, "I shouldn't have asked. If you'd rather not, I'll understand."

"What will you understand?"

"That Mr. President would rather not date a waitress."

"That's ridiculous. What you do for a living doesn't have anything to do with my decision to see you again. There's nothing wrong with being a waitress."

"Next, I guess you'll be telling me your best friend married one?" she said in an attempt at levity, meant to ease her own tension.

"No, he married an oil heiress. They're divorced now. But that has nothing to do with us. What I'm trying to say is that I would like to see you again, but I'm not certain I'll be able to make it next Thursday. What time did you have in mind?"

"If you like picnics, come at noon. If you don't, I'll cook dinner here—but I've promised myself a drive in the mountains. I love fall colors."

"So do I. I haven't been on a picnic in a long time. If I can make it then, should I bring anything?"

Her eyes sparkled with amusement. "You bring the caviar. I'll supply the peanut butter and jelly."

With a chuckle, he made his way to the door. "I'll call you soon and let you know if I can make it then. I do want to see you again, and I'm sure we can work something out."

Amaris closed the door behind him and leaned her forehead against the cool wood. She had been so afraid he would laugh at her for inviting him or that he would tell her that picnics were beneath his dignity. And he hadn't been put off by her revelation that she had The Gift. Maybe that wouldn't be a problem after all. But what about the difference in their social classes? Only time would tell about that.

Chapter Three

Amaris changed clothes three times before noon, and she would have changed again, but the sound of a car pulling up in her drive signaled her that she'd run out of time. Leaning on her dresser she stared at her reflection. Her eyes were large with apprehension and her skin looked as pale as she felt. When the doorbell sounded she patted her cheeks to bring color back to them. "It's only a date," she murmured to herself as she went to answer it. "It's only a date."

And to think she'd almost blown the chance to see him again. As he had promised, Blake called her, but instead of confirming their date for the following Thursday he told her he was scheduled to leave town Wednesday evening and wouldn't be back until late on Sunday. His tone was brusque and he seemed agitated. Her first thought was that he had changed his mind about seeing her again, and she was so absorbed with finding a response that would alleviate both his embarrassment and her own that she missed his next several sentences. When he asked her when her next day off would be, she answered that it would be Friday of the following week, and before she could say anything else he said he'd call her back and had hung up.

Ten minutes later her phone rang, but she didn't answer it, and after it quit ringing she took it off the hook. She'd been mulling over the bits and pieces of their brief conversation, and the thing that had stood out in her mind was that he couldn't be with her because he had to go bird-hunting. Clearly his hunting trip, which he had not mentioned aloud, was a higher priority to him than a picnic with her, and if that's the way things were going to be she wasn't interested.

She struggled all evening to deny the disappointment she felt, and found little solace in sleep as she dreamed that she and Blake were lovers, but that he had left her bed to go hunting—and the prey he stalked was his former fiancée, Darla Radborne.

The next morning at work she could hardly keep her eyes open, that is until she saw Blake's butler, Spenser, come through the front door. He offered Blake's apology for not coming in person, then handed her a note, saying he had been instructed to wait for her reply. She offered Spenser a seat at one of her empty tables, but he said he'd prefer to stand. Rather than suffer the indignation of reading Blake's kiss-off letter in front of his butler, Amaris excused herself and went into the back room. Vacillating between anger and disappointment, she tore open the linen envelope. As she read, tears gathered in her eyes, but they were not tears of sadness; she could hardly believe what she was reading. Blake reiterated his apology that a hunting trip his campaign manager had scheduled with some contributors to his campaign would prevent him from picnicking with her on Thursday. He said he had to do some juggling of events for the following week, but he now had Friday free and was looking forward to being with her. He said he'd tried to call but her phone seemed to be out of order, and he asked that she confirm their date by sending a note back with Spenser, rather than calling, since he would be away from the phone and didn't want to miss word from her.

Although he'd simply signed the note, Blake, the way he'd worded his message seemed sincere—almost affectionate. She'd been so foolish to jump to the wrong conclusion. After looking about for something to write on and finding only the café's order pads, Amaris turned Blake's note over and penned the words, "Looking forward to seeing you at my house at noon, Friday, the eighteenth. Amaris."

HAVING TO WAIT TO SEE Blake again had been sheer torment, and nerve-wracking, to boot. But now he was here.

"Am I too early?" Blake asked as she let him in. He was dressed in jeans and a fisherman-knit sweater and was devastatingly handsome.

"No, no. Come in. I have everything ready." As he stepped past her into the room, she couldn't help but notice the way the denim stretched tightly across his firm derriere. When he turned to face her, she realized she was staring at him and quickly averted her eyes. Crossing to the kitchen counter, she picked up the picnic hamper, resisting the urge to wipe her damp palms on her jeans because she knew Blake was following her every move. Suddenly, being alone with him in her house seemed too intimate. As she headed for the door, Blake reached out to take the basket from her and their fingers touched. A tingle raced up her arm, and as her eyes met his she felt an almost irresistible urge to kiss him. He seemed to be in no rush to move his hand away, and although she wanted to prolong the touch she knew she was sometimes too impulsive, so she released the basket. "I'll drive," she said, as she picked up her purse and began digging for her keys.

"You're in quite a hurry," he observed.

"You know how it is on your day off," she said a bit too brightly. "I don't want to waste a minute." Her face grew thoughtful. "Or maybe you don't know about days off."

"As a matter of fact, since my campaigning began I've had very little time to myself. But my guess is that you weren't referring to that. It may surprise you, but I have a job. My whole life hasn't been spent in idleness."

"I didn't mean to imply that."

"When I was a teenager, I worked at one of my father's construction companies. After college I hired on as a crewman on a yacht."

"Oh?"

"I liked it so well I bought the cruise line." He grinned down at her. "I'm kidding. I'm actually an attorney."

Amaris smiled uncertainly. She felt completely out of her element and uneasy that her attraction to him was stronger than she had felt for any man, especially for having known him such a short time. "Maybe this picnic isn't a good idea. I mean, we have nothing at all in common."

"How do you know? We've barely gotten to know each other. Are you reading my mind or something?"

The mellow resonance of his voice was disarming, and her smile became more genuine. "Of course not."

"Well, maybe you'll be surprised. Besides, we don't want to waste a single minute of your day off. Come on."

Feeling more at ease with Blake, Amaris preceded him out the door, pressing the lock button in the doorknob as she passed, and Blake pulled the door shut behind them, locking it. "Let's go in my car," he said. "I have this thing about driving."

"Hey, we do have something in common," she exclaimed. "So do I."

"I'll flip for it," he said as he pulled a quarter out of his pocket.

A few minutes later she was comfortably seated within the glove-leather interior of Blake's car, enjoying herself as she rarely did with someone else behind the wheel. Blake proved to be a safe if somewhat exuberant driver, and although he seemed to be as familiar with the mountain roads here as she was, she was more than a little amazed when he pulled into a small parking area adjacent to a group of picnic tables that overlooked the valley and announced that he felt this spot would be ideal for them.

"Did you pick this place at random?" she asked.

"Not really. I drive up here to think."

"It's pretty far from your house to be a favorite thinking spot."

"Some of my thoughts require distance."

She got out and retrieved the picnic basket from the back seat, and as she put it on one of the tables, she said, "You aren't going to believe this, but this is one of my favorite places. I often come here to watch the sunrise."

"You're kidding!"

"No, I really do."

"I mean the part about sunrise. I always assumed the sun popped up out of nowhere sometime around noon."

"You're a night person?"

"I've often wondered if I might be part vampire."

"I'm a morning person."

"That explains why I've never seen you here."

Amaris unpacked the lunch she had prepared, as Blake brought an ice chest from the trunk of his car. "I made plenty," she said as he opened it. "Fried chicken, potato salad, chips, even some brownies."

Blake grinned as he lifted out a covered silver dish and two silver spoons. "I was asked to bring caviar."

"You didn't! Caviar?"

He whisked away the lid in a dramatic flourish. "Russian. The very best."

"It looks a little like lumpy grape jelly."

"Personally I think grape jelly tastes better." He spooned some of the expensive delicacy onto a small party cracker and fed it to her.

She wrinkled her nose. "I guess it's an acquired taste."

"Caviar is better with wine." He reached back into the ice chest and produced a wine bottle and two crystal glasses wrapped in linen napkins.

"You really picnic in style."

He poured them each a glass and handed her one. "I wasn't sure if Chablis went with the peanut-butter-and-jelly sandwiches you said you'd bring, and my butler was no help on the question, so I took a chance."

"And then I didn't bring the sandwiches."

"That's okay. I know Chablis goes with chicken."

They sat side by side as they ate, and gazed out over the silent mountains. "It's always so peaceful here,"

Blake commented. "I love these mountains. Whenever I'm away on travel I miss them and can't wait to see them again."

"Do you really?"

"Don't you?"

"I've rarely been away from them. I guess that seems odd to you."

"Not really. Do you wish it did?" When she looked at him questioningly, he said, "You seem determined to find ways of pointing out our differences. Why is that?"

"I could say the same about you. Caviar and silver on a picnic?"

"That was all in fun. If I hadn't been trying to impress you, I would have just had my cook toss a couple of sandwiches in a lunch bag." He winked at her.

"Are you ever serious?"

"Usually. But for some reason you bring out the side of me most people never see. I feel I can talk to you and be myself. Doesn't that seem odd to you?"

"No." A smile tilted her lips as she bit into a brownie. "I feel the same way about you."

"Why do you suppose that is? I never felt this comfortable with Darla, and she was ready for me to run for the presidency."

"Maybe you don't really want to be president."

He looked at her as if that thought had never crossed his mind.

Once they were finished eating and she had put the remains of their meal in the basket, she led him down the slope to a huge boulder that jutted out of the mountainside. Amaris stepped onto the rock's flat surface and sat on its edge, with her feet dangling into space.

"I see fear of heights isn't one of your problems," he said as he sat beside her.

"Heights must not bother you, either," she observed.

"This boulder has been here as long as the mountain has. I doubt it will roll down to the valley today." He gazed at the hazy depths far below them, clearly deep in thought. After a while he said, "Problems seem so small up here. I look out on the valley and the mountains beyond, and I see how changeless it is. It helps keep matters in perspective."

She nodded, feeling truly comfortable with him for the first time. "When I look at this I feel a closeness with the pioneers and think how awesome it must have seemed to them. And to the Indians who were here so long before them. I'm part Indian, you know, as well as part pioneer. I have a foot in each camp, I guess you could say."

"So that's why your coloring is so unusual."

"Is it? Unusual, I mean?"

"Perhaps dramatic is a better word. Now that you mention it, I had noticed the Indian ancestry in your hair, but I admit your light eyes and fair skin led me to think otherwise. Do you think of yourself as more Indian or pioneer?"

"I think my Indian blood won out. I have no desire to conquer the wilderness. I would rather be a part of it. That's one reason I built a log cabin for my house."

"And the other?"

"It's practical and well-insulated," she said with a flash of white teeth. "I'm not fond of freezing in our winters. My friend Grace has a conventional frame house, and she has to fight icy drafts from first snowfall to spring thaw."

"I never thought about that."

"No, I don't suppose you've ever had a reason to."

He wasn't sure whether the barb was intentional, so he chose to ignore it. "What do you do when you aren't working or going on picnics?"

"Sometimes I visit with Grace and her two boys, or we go shopping in Roanoke. And I do volunteer work."

"Oh? What kind?"

"And I write magazine articles and make crafts during the winter months while I'm on leave from the café."

"What kind of volunteer work?" he prompted.

"I work with one of the local police officers, giving programs on child safety at the elementary schools."

He studied her thoughtfully for a minute. "You said you used psychometry to find me. How do you do it? I've never met anyone who does this kind of thing."

"I'm not really sure how it works, only that it does. Often I get information from holding a piece of someone's clothing or something else which they have handled. I start seeing pictures in my mind, and they are often accurate."

"Fascinating. I have heard of the police in some of the major cities asking psychics for help. Have you ever worked with the authorities?"

"I would have no idea how to approach the police with such a suggestion. They would probably think I'm crazy. Besides, I'm not right a hundred percent of the time. Psychometry and telepathy aren't that precise. What if I made a mistake on something as important as, say, a murder? No, I've never tried that. Most people have no idea I can do any of this. On the other hand, I don't think any gift is lightly bestowed, whether it's ESP or a fine singing voice or the ability to make a comfortable home. People with talents have a responsibility to use them."

"Explain."

"It's cause and effect. Whatever we put out, we get back. If I go around complaining that people are ripping me off, they probably will. If I hurt someone, I will eventually be hurt in return. But the same is true if I help someone or make life easier or more enjoyable for another person."

"That sounds too simple."

"Who said life has to be complicated to be true?"

"If everybody really believed they would receive exactly what they give to each other, the whole world would change," he mused.

Amaris only smiled.

"You've given me a lot to think about."

"You really are open-minded, aren't you?" she said as she looked into his eyes. "You aren't saying you are, just to humor me. You do intend to think about it."

"Mind-reading again?"

This time she nodded. "If you were lying to me or laughing at me I would need to know."

"Why?"

"Because today is special. You're special."

"A statement like that on a first date would make most men run for the hills."

"I wouldn't have said it to someone who would do a thing like that and, no, I didn't say it so you would respond in kind."

"I thought you just said it all works that way."

"It does, but showing a kindness to one person doesn't mean you'll receive it back from that person.

You may get your kindness returned from someone else altogether."

"You know, I really like you." He gazed deep into her eyes as if he were searching her soul."

"I like you, too, Blake."

"That's the first time you've said my name." He leaned nearer and cupped her face in his palm, then slowly stroked his thumb over her chin.

Amaris held her breath as she saw his eyes darken to the hue of pine needles. He was so close she could see the blue flecks in his eyes and each silky black eyelash. As he leaned even nearer, she closed her eyes and swayed toward him.

His lips were warm and sensuous upon hers, and his breath was sweet in her mouth. She could feel the steady beat of his heart beneath her palms as she ran her hands across his chest. His arms encircled her and cradled her close.

Her breath quickened as his kiss became more intense. The world seemed to dip and rock beneath her, and she was becoming light-headed and unsure she could retain her balance. This was all happening too fast. Gently but firmly she drew away from him.

"What's wrong?"

She refused to meet his eyes. "I'm confused. Maybe this was a mistake."

"What are you saying, Amaris? That you won't see me again?"

"No," she whispered. "I don't mean that. I don't know what I mean. I'm all mixed up inside. I have to think about this and it's getting late. Perhaps you'd better take me home."

"Of course. But I would like to see you again."

"Why?"

"Because I enjoy being with you. Your philosophy makes me think and I like that. You are interested in things more meaningful than who is dating whom or what someone was wearing the last time you saw her."

Amaris figured the last reference had to do with his former fiancée. "Are you positive you and Darla are through? I don't poach."

"We're through all right. As you intuited, she has found someone else. What Darla and I had is finished." Blake sounded a bit defensive, as if he wasn't completely certain that was true.

"I just wanted to be sure I wasn't a substitute for her affection or a diversion to help you forget her. After all, she was the one who broke up with you, and it was only a short time ago," Amaris reminded him.

"Believe me, Amaris, if I still loved her I would be fighting to get her back."

She smiled. "In that case, I'm off after next Saturday. In fact, my time will be my own for the next several months, starting next Sunday. The café is open through the winter, but business is slow, so I take a leave of absence until spring."

"Will you see me Sunday?"

Slowly Amaris nodded. "I'll be looking forward to it."

BLAKE WAS WHISTLING as he went up the steps of his mansion and let himself in the side door. Spenser seemed to materialize out of nowhere.

"Mr. Hancock is in the den, sir. I told him you might be late, but he said he would wait."

"Thank you, Spenser," Blake said as he turned toward the den. He hadn't been surprised to see Jeff's car out front. Since Jeff Hancock had taken the job as

Blake's campaign manager, he had practically taken up residence at Eventide. He was a tireless worker, often pushing both of them harder than Blake thought was necessary. Blake found his friend shooting pool.

"Hi, Blake. I hope you don't mind my waiting for you. I thought I'd come by and we could shoot a little pool and swap a few lies. This is strictly a social call. No business tonight."

"Not at all. You're always welcome here."

Jeff racked the balls as Blake took a pool cue from the wall rack. "I'm glad to see you're dating again. I was afraid you might get depressed over this thing with Darla. Is she anybody I know?"

"I doubt it." He bent over the table and sent the balls flying with his break shot. "Her name is Amaris Channing."

"Channing? You're right. I don't know her. Is she new in town?"

"She doesn't live in Roanoke. She's from Chinquapin."

"That little town off the parkway near Mabry Mill? How did you meet her?"

Blake smiled. "It was just one of those chance meetings. She's nothing at all like Darla, but I think you'll like her."

Jeff sent the three ball into the corner pocket. "Speaking of Darla, I saw her with her new boyfriend. He's several inches shorter than she is and quite a bit older."

"I know. I've met him."

"I'm glad you're taking it so well."

"Meeting Amaris helped."

"Was she at that black-tie dinner the Beauchamps gave last month?"

"No."

"She lives in Chinquapin? I didn't know anyone in our crowd was from there."

"As far as I know, none of them is."

Jeff missed his shot and frowned. "Then who is she?"

"She works at the Mountain View Café. She's a waitress." He ignored the grimace on Jeff's face.

"A what?"

"You heard me."

Jeff put down his pool cue and blatantly stared as if he thought Blake had lost his mind. "You can't date a waitress."

"I certainly can. I just did. And she has agreed to go out with me next Sunday, as well. If you've added anything to my schedule for that day since I last looked, cancel it."

"I can't believe what I'm hearing." Jeff ran his hand over his short-cropped brown hair and began to chuckle. "I get it—you're putting me on."

"No, I'm not." Blake's countenance became dark and foreboding.

Jeff's laughter abruptly ceased. "Hey, pal. I meant no offense. It's just that I was . . . surprised. I expected you'd date someone more like Darla. That's all. Your shot."

"Jeff, the last thing I want or need is another Darla. As for Amaris, you'll see what I mean when you meet her." With sure, clean movements Blake sank each of the remaining balls in rapid succession.

GRACE GLARED AT HER ex-husband and her long nails tapped reflexively on the arm of the chair. "You can see the boys here, but I'm not going to let them go to your house."

"You have no right to do this," Lyle growled. "I have visitation rights and you can't stop me!"

"Yes, I can. Until you pay the child support you owe me you aren't due any rights, as far as I'm concerned."

"That's not what the court ruled. You have to let me see my sons."

"You can see them. You just can't take them out of my house. Who knows what they might see if they go to *your* house!"

"Quit insulting me! You know I wouldn't do anything to hurt the boys."

"I know no such thing! You're the one who left us to shack up with that bimbo!"

"Tiffany is no bimbo!"

"She certainly is! She wrecked our marriage!"

Lyle drew a breath in an obvious effort to calm himself. "So I made a mistake. One lousy mistake! Tiffany and I are no longer together. I'm not even dating anyone right now."

Grace was trying hard to contain her anger. "That isn't the point. You owe me four months of child support!"

"I'm out of work, damn it! As I told you before, I didn't quit my job just so I wouldn't have to send you the money."

"I'm still not convinced of that."

Lyle stood and paced angrily to the window. "Quit pushing me, Grace. One of these days you're going to push me too far."

"Oh? Well, you've already done that to me. You went way too far when you left me for that...that child!"

"She's not a child!"

Grace saw a movement in the doorway and turned to find Todd and Ben standing there. How much had they heard? she wondered. At nine and seven years of age, respectively, they would understand what she was talking about. "I didn't hear you two come in from school," she said with forced cheerfulness.

"We just got here. Hi, Dad," Todd said, as he looked anxiously from one parent to he other.

"Hi, Daddy," Ben echoed. "Want to see the picture I drew in school?"

Grace tried to restrain her temper as Lyle knelt to inspect his younger son's artwork, and her voice held a nervous edge as she said, "There are cookies in the jar and milk in the refrigerator."

"In a minute," Todd said. "Dad, I've decided to try out for the football team at school when I'm old enough. Will you show me how to throw a football so it goes straight?"

Grace stood and glared at her ex-husband over her son's head. "Your father doesn't know the first thing about football, Todd."

"As a matter of fact, I do," Lyle corrected her icily. "Let's go out back and play a quick game."

The boys whooped and tumbled over each other in their eagerness to comply. While they charged up to their room to get the football, Grace said, "Don't you get their hopes up about going to visit you at your apartment. And if they bring it up, don't fill their heads full of lies about it being my fault. It's your fault and you know it!"

"Damn you, Grace. You aren't going to come between me and my boys." He stepped closer and added. "As for Tiffany and myself, you might spend some time asking yourself why I had to look elsewhere for female companionship. I might have done wrong, but I wasn't the only one at fault. Not many men would have put up with you for as long as I did."

Grace caught her breath and turned away before he could see the tears in her eyes. "Get out of my sight," she ground out through clenched teeth.

"Gladly!"

She heard Lyle slam out the back door, and in a few minutes she heard the boys race out after him. Grace drew a kitchen chair up to the window and sat in the shadows to watch them at play. How had her life fallen apart so miserably? She and Lyle had had so much going for them in the beginning. When the boys were born she had been happier than she had ever thought she could be. She had lavished love on them and worked herself sick to keep the house, hold down a job and tend to them. It wasn't her fault if there weren't enough hours in a day for her to give Lyle the amount of attention he had had before the babies came. It wasn't her fault that she had always been so tired at night or that she had lost interest in lovemaking because of it. Anybody who worked as hard as she did would be exhausted at the end of the day.

She watched Lyle throw the football to Todd and wondered what she had ever seen in him to love. Whatever it had been, it was indiscernible to her now.

Chapter Four

"You wouldn't believe what Lyle did Thursday night," Grace complained, as she and Amaris straightened up the café at closing time. "He came over and was teaching the boys how to play football. As if he knew anything at all about it. He even used to sleep through the games on TV."

Amaris wisely made no comment.

Grace continued. "And he kept them out there in the yard until pitch-dark. I had to wait supper on them. On a school night, too! Ben was so wound up, he was an hour late falling asleep."

"It won't hurt him to stay up late once in a while, will it?"

"That's not the point. Lyle thinks he can sail in and out of our lives and be as disruptive as he pleases. *He* wasn't the one who had to talk Ben into going to bed. *He* doesn't have to worry whether or not they do well in school. I'll bet Ben can hardly keep his eyes open all day."

"Maybe so, but isn't it good for the boys to know their father still cares about them and wants to spend time with them?" Amaris placed the salt-and-pepper shakers on a tray, along with the ketchup and steak-sauce bottles, and carried them to the kitchen so they could be refilled.

"Lyle only cares about himself," Grace said as she followed Amaris into the kitchen.

"You didn't tell the boys that, did you?"

"No, but sometimes I'm tempted." Grace started washing the tops of the ketchup bottles.

"You know you shouldn't. That would be terribly traumatic to them, to think Lyle doesn't love them. Besides, if it were true, he wouldn't try to spend so much time with them."

"Amaris, you can be so naive. He does it just to irritate me. He's probably brainwashing them against me."

Amaris looked up from her work. "Come on now, Grace. You know better than that."

"No, I don't. You should have seen how surly Todd was after Lyle left. He wanted us all to have supper together and I'll bet anything Lyle put him up to it."

Amaris went back to filling the pepper shakers.

"You can't know what it's like to get a divorce, unless you've been through one. It certainly brought out Lyle's true colors!"

"Grace, I'm your friend and you know I care for you, but when it comes to the subject of Lyle you're just plain bitter."

"I have every right to be! Amaris, you know what all I lived through with that man. Remember the time he threatened to have me committed to a mental hospital?" Grace looked about, to be sure their boss wasn't within earshot. You know, because of my interest in psychic things. Like telepathy and all that."

"As I recall, that was during the heat of an argument you two were having."

"I know, but if I hadn't tried to convince him I have some psychic abilities, he would have had one less thing to hold over my head. He even told the boys it was all a bunch of nonsense, and I think Todd believed him."

Amaris had run into this prejudice often herself and she knew it was real. She also knew how devastating it could be to the victim.

"And remember, during the divorce when he decided he was going to try to get custody of the boys and I told him if he did I'd name Tiffany McNee as his mistress in court, he said he'd tell the court about my belief in psychic things and prove I wasn't a fit mother."

"But then his attorney convinced him to drop the whole idea."

"And you kept me from going to pieces worrying about it until he did. I don't know what I'd have done without you. The only reason he tried to get custody in the first place was to hurt me."

"Are you sure? I really do think he loves the boys."

"I suppose he does, but Amaris, he's got a mean streak in him I didn't know was there."

"I find that hard to believe. I've known you two for years, and Lyle didn't seem like that at all."

"You never know what a person is like until you live with him."

Amaris put the pepper shakers back on the tray and started filling the salt. As a telepathist she was rarely wrong about people, but divorce was tremendously stressful. And stress sometimes changed people's behavior.

"I'm going to miss seeing you every day," Grace said, changing the subject. "It gets so dreary in here during the winter. There are barely enough customers to warrant Frank staying open at all. Thank goodness he does, though. I couldn't go several months without a paycheck.''

''Will you let me buy coats for the boys? I have some extra money saved.''

''That's really sweet of you, but as I've said before, it's Lyle's responsibility to see that they are taken care of and I'm going to see that he does it. Besides, I can afford it, if it comes to that. It's the principal of the thing.''

Again Amaris held her tongue. Grace frequently put the boys in the middle of her war with Lyle, and although Amaris wished she could reason her out of it, she knew it would only cause a problem between her and Grace if she mentioned it. The best thing she could do was to maintain the friendship until Grace got her wits about her again.

Apparently Grace noticed Amaris's silence and got the subtle message. Changing the subject, she asked, ''What are you planning to do next week?''

''Bridget Wiley and I have an appointment at the kindergarten, to tell the children and their parents about safety rules. You know—don't ride with strangers, don't leave school with anyone except your parents. That sort of thing. You remember Bridget, don't you? She was the lady from the police department who was with me when I did this same talk to Ben's kindergarten class.''

''Sure I do. That was when Ben memorized our phone number and learned how to use a pay phone and how to call the operator to get help.''

''Then, I suppose I'll get started on some of my crafts.''

"That's not really what I was asking," Grace playfully chided. "I want to know when you will be seeing Blake Mayfield again."

"Tomorrow." Amaris's lips tilted up in a smile. "I can't wait for you to meet him."

"Too bad I have to work tomorrow. Maybe you could come by for dessert or something."

"You wouldn't have a chance to visit with him then. You know how Frank is about us talking to the customers for any length of time. I'll plan for us to all get together one day soon when you aren't at the café."

"Sounds like you plan to keep him around."

"Long enough to get to know him. He's different from anyone I've ever met."

"You're probably different from anyone he's ever met, too. Did you ever tell him how you knew who he was?"

"It sort of slipped out, and I was really surprised he took it so well. I don't know if I was subconsciously trying to run him off or what, but before I had thought much about it I was giving him a demonstration by reading a key chain he was carrying. He's really open-minded about such things."

"I hope he stays that way. Sometimes people change. Especially after marriage."

Amaris laughed. "Marriage? Why, I barely know him." But she had daydreamed about falling in love with him, so she added, "What do you think about us? Blake and myself, I mean. Do you think we could work out anything lasting? Our backgrounds are hardly the same."

"You just aim for the diamonds on the left hand, and you can work out the details later."

"Grace, that's a terrible thing to say. I'm interested in Blake, not his money."

"His money doesn't hurt. Take it from me—if you have a choice, go for the gold. Scrimping and scraping to make ends meet is no fun." Grace loaded the condiments back on the tray and returned them to the dining room. "I'm not saying a person ought to marry only for money, but you have to look ahead these days."

"He's campaigning for governor," Amaris said, as she straightened the chairs at each table.

"Frank told me. Most of the Mayfield family have been in politics, so I'm not surprised. I remember studying about Richard L. Mayfield in my government class in school. Whoever would have guessed I might meet one of his descendants? Or that I might know a future wife of a governor?"

"Even if we were that serious about each other, I'm not at all sure I would want to be a governor's wife."

"Why not? All those parties and jet-setting around. I'd grab at the chance."

"I wouldn't know the first thing about that sort of life. I'm not sure I would fit in. Besides, a politician's wife should be a socialite or from an influential family. Being a waitress at the Mountain View Café is hardly the same. No, I'd never do at all."

"Sounds like your trying to convince yourself," Grace said.

Amaris didn't answer, because she knew Grace was right.

After the restaurant was ready for the next day's customers, Amaris and Grace let themselves out the back door and locked up. Amaris handed her friend her key. "Will you give this to Frank? I may not see him for a few days, and you know how nervous he gets about keys being loose."

"Sure thing." Grace threaded Amaris's restaurant key onto the chain next to her own key. "Why not come over to the house for a while? It's still early. The boys were saying this morning that they haven't seen you in days."

"I guess I could for a little while. I need to wash some clothes before I go to bed tonight, but I can do that later."

Grace's small but neat wood-frame house was in an older residential neighborhood just north of Chinquapin's downtown. Grace had once commented that she and Lyle could have afforded a nicer house but had chosen this one because it was within easy walking distance of the boys' elementary school. Grace's children truly were the center of her life and Amaris wondered if she would feel that way toward her own children some day. Grace briskly led the way up the back steps, but abruptly stopped when she found the door was unlocked. As a frown darkened her face she stepped inside, calling, "Todd? Why is this door open? I've told you a dozen times to keep it locked."

"Sorry, Mom," he said as he poked his head around the corner. When he saw who had come home with his mother, he grinned and added, "Hi, Aunt Amaris."

"Hi, Todd." Although Amaris was not related to them, she was there so often, they referred to her as if she were. "Where's Ben?"

"He says he's doing schoolwork, but it just looks like coloring to me," Todd answered with the maturity of a veteran fourth-grader.

"Speaking of homework, do you have any?" Grace asked as she hung her coat and Amaris's on the hat tree.

"Nobody has homework over the weekend," Todd said. "It's against the rules or something."

"That's news to me. Amaris, how about a soft drink?"

"No, thanks." Amaris smiled as Ben came into the room. "How's my youngest fellow doing?"

"Fine," Ben said promptly. "See what I'm doing?"

Amaris praised the picture he had colored, then said, "Have you boys been practicing what I taught you last time?"

"I have," Ben announced. "I can consecrate real good."

"Concentrate," Amaris corrected with a laugh. "It's very important because that way if you ever get lost in the woods, you'll be better able to find your way out."

"I never get lost," Todd said.

"I know a boy who's getting too big for his britches," his mother remarked in a mock warning.

"Well, I don't. I know these woods as well as I know our yard."

"Just to be on the safe side, though, you need to know how to center yourself and to visualize your surroundings and the path you took getting there."

"I can do it," Ben piped up. "Want to see me?"

"Sure, I do. Go in your room and show me something," Amaris said.

Ben ran away to do what she said. Todd frowned down at his tennis shoes. "Don't you want to try it, Todd?" Amaris asked.

"No, I don't believe in it." He glanced quickly at the adults to see what they thought about this. "There's no such thing as mind-reading."

"Now I wonder where you heard that," Grace remarked dryly. "You sound like a recording of your father."

"The kids at school don't believe in it, either," Todd said defensively. "Quit blaming everything on Dad."

Amaris put her arm around Todd's shoulder. "Will you go get me a glass of water?"

Grudgingly he went to the kitchen.

"You won't get anywhere by making him choose sides, Grace."

"I know it, but it makes me so mad. Anything Lyle says is fact, and everything I say is wrong."

Amaris sat in a chair and let her mind become receptive. After a while she said, "Does Ben have a rabbit up there?"

"Not as far as I know."

"I keep seeing a rabbit."

In a few minutes Ben came racing downstairs with a gray bear under his arm. "Did you see it, Aunt Amaris? Did you see it?"

"I saw a rabbit. What were you thinking about?"

Ben's small face fell and he held up the bear. "This."

"That's a new one, isn't it? I don't think I've met this bear."

"Dad gave it to me." Ben glanced apprehensively at his mother. "I named him Bugs."

Amaris laughed. " I guess that explains why I saw a rabbit. I'd say you did a fine job, Ben." She looked up as Todd brought her the glass of water. The censure on his face spoke volumes.

Grace sent the boys outside to play. "You see what I mean? Lyle says he can't pay child support or buy them coats, but he has money to buy Ben a toy. Todd probably got one, too, but you can bet he won't tell me. And when do you suppose Lyle gave it to them? He didn't do it last Thursday. That means he must have been here while I was at work." She paced to the window and glared out at the darkness. "Damn! That makes me so mad!"

Amaris felt sorry that Grace was clinging so tightly to her negative feelings but knew better than to point it out to her. Choosing to appeal to Grace's logic, Amaris said, "Aren't you glad he checks up on the boys? I know you worry about them coming home to an empty house."

"I don't want my ex-husband snooping around in here while I'm gone!"

"But, Grace—"

"No, I'm right about this one. Lyle has no right to come in here while I'm not home."

"You don't know that he did," Amaris reminded her. "He may have merely dropped off a toy and left again."

"I wish he had dropped off some winter coats! Or better yet, that he had dropped completely off the earth."

Amaris finished off her glass of water and stood up. Grace was in no mood to listen to anything. "I had better be going. You'll want to start supper."

"I'm sorry, Amaris," Grace said with regret. "I really am. It's just that where Lyle is concerned, I can't be rational. Or even civil, it would seem."

"That's okay. I really do need to be going."

"You won't stay for supper? I promise not to mention the enemy."

"Thanks, but not tonight."

She told the boys goodbye and drove away through the narrow streets, thankful for the silvery glow from the rising full moon. Normally at night the valley was velvety black, the sheltering mountains blocking even the light from the stars, except those directly overhead. Sometimes the narrow valley in which Chinquapin was located closed in on her, making her feel a bit claustrophobic, and she wondered if it might have felt that way to some of the people who settled it. Had it not been for having to negotiate the winding roads in the winter, she would have chosen to live on the slopes of the mountain so she could enjoy a panoramic view.

That thought reminded her of Blake's house. He had a lovely view of the valley beyond the mountain to the northwest. He could probably see the colors of sunset from his porch. Here in her valley, both sunset and dawn came only as a pale light from behind the crests of the mountains. That was why in fair weather she drove up the winding road to see the colors. She liked Chinquapin, for it was her home, but it had its drawbacks.

As she parked at her house, she heard the phone ringing and hurried inside to answer it.

"I was beginning to think you weren't coming home," Blake's voice said in response to her breathless hello.

"I just got in. I went by Grace's house after work." Hearing his voice gave her a warm feeling all over.

"I wanted to ask if you'd like to have dinner in Roanoke tomorrow night. My friend Jeff Hancock asked if we would like to join him and his date for dinner."

"He knows about me?"

"I told him about you."

Amaris wished she knew what he had said about her, but her sense of ethics prevented her from probing his mind to find out. "Sure. I hadn't planned for us to do anything in particular."

"Okay, I'll call him and tell him to expect us. Do you like Greek food?"

"I have no idea."

"He has reservations at the Athena Restaurant. Unless you'd rather not."

"That's fine with me." She wondered what she should wear to this place, never having heard of it before. Her wardrobe was rather limited. He'd mentioned reservations, and that indicated it wasn't one of Roanoke's more casual restaurants. Nonetheless, the best she had would have to do, and surely Blake would have assumed that she had no formal attire—or at least she hoped he had. "What time will you pick me up?"

"How about seven o'clock? The reservation is for eight, and that will give us plenty of time to drive to Roanoke."

"Okay. I'll be ready at seven." She said goodbye and hung up. She knew that Jeff Hancock was not only Blake's friend but his campaign manager as well. What if the man had extended the invitation in order to "audition" Blake's new girlfriend? she wondered, then chided herself for being so suspicious of someone she'd never met. She'd been listening to too much of Grace's paranoia of late. Still, it was important that she leave a favorable impression on Blake's friends, so she made a mental note that Blake had referred to the meal as "dinner" rather than "supper." She would have to be careful to call it dinner, since that was their custom.

When she realized the lengths she was going to, so as not to embarrass herself or Blake and his friends, she became exasperated. Talking to herself, she said, "I'm not cut out for this." She had never tried to be anything other than herself, and she didn't like the feeling that she might inadvertently say or do something awkward. All at once she wished she had had the nerve to ask what sort of clothes were appropriate to wear to that restaurant.

Amaris started her wash, then made supper and ate it as she watched TV. Although the sitcom she had chosen was one of her favorites, she was paying little attention to the show. Instead she was wondering if Blake ate off silver and china when he was alone, or if he ever just opened a can of soup and kicked back. Probably not, she decided, since he had mentioned having a cook. Yet Blake didn't seem to be terribly formal.

After she washed and dried the dishes, Amaris pulled on a heavy sweater and went out onto the long, narrow patio deck out back that stretched from the house to just beyond the edge of the stream. As she passed by a patio chair, she grabbed one of the cushions and carried it with her to the far end of the deck where she tossed it down and then sat on it, comfortably crossing her legs beneath her.

The moon was fully visible now, having crested the mountaintop in its journey across the crisp autumn sky. Not a single star could compete with its brilliance. Beneath her, she could hear the rush of waters that splashed over the silvered rapids nearby. Amaris rested her hands lightly on her knees, palms up. Keeping her spine straight, she leveled her chin and began to breathe with a measured cadence that would take her into deep relaxation.

Amaris often sat here in the moonlight, weather permitting. Being alone with her thoughts helped her sort things out and maintain a generally positive outlook on life. And afterward she always felt energized and invigorated. By freeing her mind from the bounds of logic and reasoning, she was often able to find solutions to the most complex questions in her life. And the most effective way she'd found to release her thoughts was by using her imagination to take her far away from the real world. Often her imagination seemed to have a mind of its own. With the slow release of another deep breath, she left all her problems and cares behind.

At first, in her mind's eye, she saw a pathway of clouds spiraling up into the silvery moonlight. With no mental effort at all, she followed it upward. At the top she stepped out onto a landscape of moon-washed billows, and as she walked ahead a crystal castle appeared before her. The door opened and she entered.

The walls, floor and ceiling were all made of glittering prisms that were simultaneously no color and all colors; the feeling there was one of warmth and serenity. She had been here before and it had always been important. In an inner room she paused. In front of her an image fancifully danced about, and as she watched it took form. It became Ben and Todd. At first they were together, then all at once Ben was gone and Todd was crouched behind something large and dark. He was crying and holding both hands over his eyes as if to shut out something that frightened him.

"What does this mean?" Amaris asked herself with mild alarm.

At that instant, several dark circles appeared over his head. "Remember," he said.

All at once Amaris was back on her deck. She hadn't been aware of the passage of time but noticed the moon had already passed behind the mountain and the ambient light was fading. She felt shaken to the core of her being, and for half an hour she tried in vain to return to the crystalline castle.

Giving up, she leaned her elbows on her knees and stared at the glistening water. Todd was safe at home. She had seen him only hours earlier. She shook her head in confusion. The vision meant nothing at all to her. Maybe it was symbolic. But she couldn't make any sense out of it from that angle, either. Deciding the answer would come to her when it was supposed to, she headed for the warmth and coziness of her cabin.

Chapter Five

Amaris couldn't decide what to wear. Her dates were rarely so formal as to preclude her wearing cotton dresses or everyday slacks. There just wasn't anyplace in Chinquapin that required dressing up. She had an uneasy feeling that the Athena Restaurant didn't fit into the same category.

After searching through her closet twice, she pulled out a pair of black slacks and a matching blouse. She had made the outfit from a silk fabric, and while it was rather lightweight for that time of year, it was flattering on her. She put on her makeup and blew her hair dry, then dressed. After tucking in her shirttail, she snapped a belt of silver conchos around her waist and fastened a curved half-moon of silver about her neck. The jewelry was inexpensive, but it was tasteful. After adding her silver earrings and her silver-and-turquoise ring, she thought she looked quite respectable.

She was putting her lipstick, comb and driver's license into her black leather handbag when she heard Blake's car drive up. Hastily she snapped the bag shut and looked in the mirror. Her raven hair swept back from her face and fell straight to her shoulders. The light gleamed in her glossy hair and glinted off her silver jewelry; her skin glowed with excitement. Then the doorbell rang and she lost all her self-confidence.

When she opened the door Blake stood there looking as elegant as a dream prince. She wanted to ask him if she was dressed appropriately, but she couldn't get the words out.

"You're beautiful," he said as he stepped into the house. "Very dramatic. I like that."

His compliment put her more at ease and she smiled. He wore a navy suit with a white shirt and a claret tie. Judging by his smile, she decided everything was all right. After all, she told herself, clothes were so unimportant when you got right down to it. The significant part of a person was on the inside. This was simply a date and she was only going to meet his friend. She could just be herself.

"You look wonderful," she said as she picked up her purse. "I like that tie."

"Thanks." He looked both surprised and pleased, as if he were unaccustomed to being complimented.

As they drove toward Roanoke, Amaris said, "Tell me about Jeff. How long have you known him?"

"All my life. My father and Jeff's father were close friends. I can't remember a time when I didn't know him. He married when he finished college, but it didn't last. He's divorced now."

"Any children?"

"No."

"My friend Grace is having all kinds of problems over the breakup of her marriage. She has two boys, ages nine and seven—really great kids. The problem is that she and her ex-husband are at war over them. He can't pay support, so she's refusing to let him have visitation."

"She can't do that."

"She's doing it."

"Why can't he pay?"

"Lyle lost his job. He worked for the highway department but was laid off a few months ago."

"Why doesn't he get another job?"

"There aren't many openings in Chinquapin, and none that he's qualified for."

"Couldn't he move to Roanoke or Richmond?"

"I guess he could, but that would take him away from the boys. If Grace won't let them visit him here in town, she sure won't let them go all the way to Richmond."

Blake's eyes never left the road ahead of them, but she sensed his irritation. "Why doesn't he get a lawyer and demand his rights?"

"If he could afford a lawyer, he could pay child support. It's a catch-22." Amaris was thoughtful for a moment. "I can see Grace's position, too. She really needs the money. On her salary alone, she can hardly make ends meet. If one of the boys gets sick or there's some unexpected expense, she will have a problem."

"Couldn't she leave town and find a better job?"

"I doubt it. Grace has never been anything but a waitress, and the pay would be the same in the city as it is here. In Chinquapin, she doesn't have to worry so much about her boys being home alone from the time school lets out until she gets off work. Of course Grace is a worrier by nature, but there's not as much reason here."

"It must be difficult to raise children alone."

"I'm sure it is. They're good boys, though. I've known them most of their lives."

Blake looked across at her as if something she had said had piqued his interest. As he eased his car onto the highway that led to Roanoke, he said, "You sound as if you like children."

"I do. Who wouldn't?"

"Darla didn't. Her grand ambitions left no room for motherhood."

"Do you want children?"

"Yes, and not just one. I found it lonely to be an only child. I want at least two."

"So do I. I don't have any brothers or sisters, either, and I've always regretted it."

"My house is too big to be comfortable as a bachelor's residence. It was designed and built for a family with children."

"It's a beautiful house."

"Thank you."

"Why do you sound as if you aren't used to receiving compliments?"

Blake thought for a minute. "Do I? I've never been aware of that."

"Did Darla pay you compliments?"

"Not very often. She wasn't the type."

Amaris thought about that for a minute. She had never considered there was a type who gave compliments and one who didn't. If she liked something she usually came right out and said so.

"I'm looking forward to your meeting Jeff," Blake said as they entered the city.

"So am I." She couldn't think of anything else to say about this meeting, because doubt that it might not go well was creeping back in. Blake and Jeff were obviously close friends, and it seemed to her that Blake put a lot of credence in Jeff's opinions. Thus, it was important that she make a good impression on Jeff, and Amaris was never at her best on first meetings. As soon as she shook hands with a person she usually knew exactly what the person was like, and this made her forget to proceed with the normal get-acquainted ritual. Therefore most people often considered her to be too familiar, or if she remembered to be careful, too cool.

Blake pulled into the parking lot of a low white building with a red tile roof. Before Amaris could open her door, it was swung open by a uniformed parking attendant. As she got out, she felt awkward and out of her element, but she was determined to make the best of it.

Blake took her inside as if he were familiar with the place from long practice. The maître d' greeted him by name, then escorted them beneath a trellis-covered archway, which had been tastefully decorated with realistic-looking vines and grapes, to the cozy dining room.

As they approached the table, Blake whispered, "Jeff has brought along Karen. I didn't expect this."

Amaris felt his apprehension and her steps slowed. The woman looked more predatory than friendly, with her carefully styled red hair, long red nails and her sequined sweater.

"Hello, Jeff, Karen," Blake said as they reached the table. "This is Amaris Channing. Amaris, Jeff Hancock and Karen Edmund."

Amaris forced a smile to her nervous lips as she held out her hand. "Hello, Karen." The woman extended her fingertips. "It's nice to meet you, Jeff." At least his handshake was firmer than that of his date. "Blake has told me so much about you."

"Oh?" Karen said, her voice low and husky as if she had chain-smoked since birth. "I don't recall that he has ever mentioned you at all."

"I haven't known her very long," Blake said to Karen as he seated Amaris opposite the woman. "I hope we haven't kept you waiting."

"We just got here," Jeff replied as he unabashedly assessed Amaris.

The waiter handed them each an oversized menu, and as Amaris read, she developed a sinking feeling. She had no idea what any of the dishes might be, and had no idea what to order. When the waiter returned to take their order, her stomach churned as if it were filled with butterflies.

Blake smiled at her. "I recommend the speciality of the house. It's a spiced meat dish."

Amaris gave him a grateful look. "That sounds good."

Blake ordered for them both, then Karen and Jeff ordered, the Greek food names tripping smoothly off their tongues.

"You must come here often," Amaris said. "You knew just what to order."

Karen and Jeff exchanged a look, then Karen said, "I've frequently summered in Greece. So have Jeff and Blake. Haven't you?"

"No. No, I've never been to Greece."

"You haven't? Where do you spend your summers?" Karen looked as if she knew the answer to that already but was displaying her claws to amuse her date.

Amaris refused to be ruffled. "In Chinquapin. I'm a waitress at the Mountain View Café." She saw Karen's eyes widen, and knew she had surprised her with her honesty. "I don't have much time for travel in the summer, and in the winter I write or make Indian crafts to sell. I'm half Indian, you see."

Karen stiffened in her chair and looked as if she had had all the honesty she could take, so Amaris finished with, "You should come to the café sometime. We don't serve fine food like this, but I guarantee you won't leave hungry."

Amaris glanced at Blake, relieved that his eyes were sparkling as if he had enjoyed seeing Karen set back on her heels.

"Why don't you tell Karen what sort of crafts you do?" Blake suggested.

"Mostly weaving. I have a loom set up in my back room. Sometimes I do bead work. I try to keep the crafts as authentic as I can, as far as design and yarns go. I buy the beads, however. It takes too long to make them by hand. But buying beads doesn't make it less authentic, for my ancestors also bought their beads from the white man."

"Do you also tan your own hides?" Karen acidly quipped.

"No, I think it's wrong to kill animals for their hides or for sport. Don't you?"

"I never thought of it one way or another," Karen replied, as if the whole subject were boring.

"I'd like to see some of your work," Blake said.

Karen leaned toward him and said with saccharin sweetness, "Maybe that's some of her work she's wearing. It is, Amaris?"

Amaris felt a blush of color rising in her cheeks. No one would ever have inferred that Karen's sequined sweater was homemade. She had no choice but to brave her way through this. "As a matter of fact, it is. At least the clothes are. One of my cousins made the jewelry. He's a silversmith.''

"An Indian silversmith? How quaint."

"He's from the other side of my family. The ones who came over on the *Mayflower.*" By Karen's slackened jaw, Amaris knew the woman's family was newer to America than her own.

Amaris was thankful when their salads soon arrived and conversation dwindled. She was determined not to let Karen see how ill-at-ease she felt and wanted nothing more than to finish this evening and never see the woman again. And maybe Jeff, too. The fact that he'd hardly spoken probably meant he shared Karen's disdain. She regretted that she hadn't read him when they shook hands, but she'd thought her nervousness might have thrown her off, if she'd tried.

"This food is good," she said to Blake. "I wonder what spices the cook uses."

"I don't know, but I could ask."

Karen sighed audibly. Amaris shook her head and said, "Never mind. I only wondered."

"Tell us about yourself," Jeff said. "Have you lived in Virginia long?"

"All my life. I graduated from the University of Virginia and went back to Chinquapin. I've been there ever since."

"You have a college degree and you're..." Jeff faltered in mid-sentence, as if he had realized the question on his tongue would be insulting.

Karen also picked up on Jeff's thought but not his manners as she finished his sentence, "...working as a waitress."

"Karen! I don't think—" Jeff began.

"I work as a waitress because I enjoy doing it."

"I think people should do whatever job they most enjoy," Blake said, on her behalf.

Karen turned to Blake. "But with a college education, she could surely get a better-paying job than that."

Amaris didn't want Blake to be put in the position of having to defend her, so she quickly responded. "I'm not interested in making more money. I'm comfortable with what I have. Besides, I enjoy visiting with the people. The Mountain View is a popular café, and during a week's time I get to see almost everyone in town at least once. Then there are the tourists. It's fascinating to know all the places they've been." Blake was smiling approval, and Jeff's jaw had gone slack.

"They tell you the stories of their travels?" Karen asked. "What an odd thing for them to do."

Amaris drew back. She had almost made a mistake. Most of the information she gleaned from the tourists was by telepathy or from psychometry when she handed them their coats or parcels. "People are friendly in Chinquapin. I guess it's something in the water," she added lightly.

"I've noticed they're special," Blake said with a grin.

Amaris gratefully returned his smile.

Jeff finally regained his tongue. "Karen, I think you'd better go powder your nose."

"But I—"

"And I'll help you," Jeff added as he rose and led her from the table.

Blake looked as if he were going to apologize for his friends' behavior, but as quickly as they'd left the table Jeff and Karen returned. Jeff nodded to Blake as if to say everything was under control, and as they finished their entrees the conversation was sparse and noncontroversial. Karen said nothing at all.

For dessert they had the traditional baklava. The flaky pastry filled with honey and minced nuts was cloyingly sweet but delicious. Amaris wished she had the recipe but refrained from saying so. She only wanted to cut the evening short and escape from this awkward situation. She had struggled so to guard her words that she felt claustrophobic.

At last the check was brought to the table, and it wasn't without effort that Amaris refrained from sighing with relief. Blake waved away Jeff's effort to pay for the meal and laid a gold credit card on the tray. The waiter silently took it away, and in moments returned for Blake's signature on the credit slip.

"This was an interesting dinner," Jeff said as the waiter handed Blake his receipt.

Karen was unable to keep quiet any longer. "Of course the Athena isn't as authentic as some I've been in, but I doubt people around here know the difference." Her eyes came to rest on Amaris, and she added, "And it is amusing."

Jeff jumped to his feet. "Would you all like to go over to my house for after-dinner drinks?"

"No, thanks," Blake said, his voice sounding as strained as Amaris felt. "We have other plans."

She could have kissed him out of gratitude.

"What do you have planned?" Karen asked.

"Karen, it's none of our business." Jeff pointed out. Karen's eyes bored through Jeff as her face flushed from her anger.

Blake stood up and held Amaris's chair. Through clenched teeth, he said, "Give me a call tomorrow."

Without more than a brief nod at Karen, Blake took Amaris away.

They were silent until they were almost out of town. "I'm sorry," he said at last.

Amaris felt hot tears rush to her eyes. "It wasn't your fault."

"Would you like to stop by Eventide for a drink?"

"No. I only want to get home."

The ride was passed in an awkward silence. Amaris felt as if she were living through a nightmare. The pale lights of Chinquapin had never looked better to her.

When Blake stopped the car at her house she reached for the door handle but Blake caught her arm. "I'm sorry for the way they acted. If I had known he was bringing Karen, I would have canceled out."

"They're your friends."

"Karen isn't. She and Darla were roommates in college, and Karen feels I should try to get Darla back. Even in our usual circle, she's known for having a malicious tongue. Everyone but Jeff avoids her."

"What could he possibly see in her?" Amaris asked in a pained voice. "She was so hateful!"

"I don't know. Jeff has appalling taste in women. Karen could almost pass as a twin for his ex-wife. He seems to need that kind of antagonism in his relationships with women."

Amaris didn't answer. She knew Blake was right. She had sensed a vacuum in Jeff's self-esteem. "I ought to feel sorry for him. I really do feel embarrassed over the way I reacted toward her."

"You shouldn't. I admired the way you handled yourself. As for Jeff...I'll talk with him tomorrow. He knew it was important to me for you two to meet. He should have had better sense than to invite Karen Edmund.''

"Why was this meeting important?" Amaris looked at him across the dark interior of the car. "I don't fit into your world, and tonight should have proved it to you. What do you want from me?"

"I don't want anything from you." He reached across the car seat and ran the back of his fingers over the petal-soft curve of her cheek.

"Come walk with me," she said.

"You'll be cold. A front is passing through."

"I'll get a wrap...unless you'd rather leave."

"I'm in no hurry." He came around and opened her door.

Amaris let herself in and took a woven shawl from the hall tree. "Come out back. I want to show you something."

He went with her out onto the deck. The water rushing beneath it sounded louder in the darkness. The moon hung full and fat overhead, waning only slightly.

"It's beautiful out here," he said.

"My grandmother used to tell me that pine trees and running water lifted one's spirits."

"My grandmother said the same thing about shopping at Saks."

"That figures." Amaris started to walk away, but Blake stopped her.

"Amaris, we knew there were differences between us from the moment we met. Can't you see these things as points of interest and not as barriers?"

"They feel like walls. I don't think anyone in my entire family has ever been inside Saks, much less gone shopping there just to raise his spirits."

"That particular grandmother was brought up in New York City. They don't have an abundance of pine trees and mountain streams there. She had to make do."

Amaris smiled faintly. After a while she said, "I would understand if you didn't want to see me again."

"My friends' rudeness has nothing to do with me."

"No? I think a person's friends are a reflection of how a person views life. Also it would put a strain on you to have your friends and me."

"I've told you Karen is not my friend. When Darla and I broke up, Karen was ready to serve my liver to the birds."

"Jeff, then. I know you care what he thinks."

"Yes...well, that's another matter. Jeff isn't just my friend, he works for me as my campaign manager."

"And that's another thing. The election is coming up soon, and I'm not sure our friendship will be an asset for you."

"I choose my own friends, and not for political reasons."

"Then you must not want very badly to be governor. I hear politicians have to be careful with whom they associate."

"I am. And if you are referring to the differences in our backgrounds, I'm sure you're more sensitive about it than anyone else is."

"I'm not so sure. Ask Karen what she thinks."

"Karen has nothing to do with this!"

"She may be more representative of 'the people' than you give her credit for!" She turned away and leaned against the rail. "What has gotten into me? We've only had two dates and here I am talking as if it

matters whether you know me or not. It's not like me
to read so much into things like this."

He came to her and drew her into his arms. "Have
we only had two dates? I feel as if I've known you forever."

Amaris pressed her cheek against the hard wall of his
chest. "I keep forgetting that we haven't, too. You're
not like anyone I've ever known. And I don't mean
your money," she added.

Slowly he rubbed his hand across her shoulders.
"There must be some way for us to work this out. This
is America. Class differences shouldn't mean anything
here."

"'Shouldn't' and 'don't' are two different matters," she replied with a sigh. "It's been a long time
since we had a rail-splitter as president."

"I don't think we are all that far apart. If we try, I'm
sure we can find a common ground."

"It won't be easy."

"You're worth whatever it takes."

"Am I?" She lifted her head to look up at him.
"Why?"

"I don't know. I know it sounds trite, but you're like
a breath of fresh air. I don't know what to expect out
of you. When I saw Karen at the table I almost turned
around and took you away. I've seen her make mince-
meat out of people with far more experience than you
have."

"Why didn't you?"

"Jeff had already seen us before I noticed Karen. I
decided to go through with it and defend you as necessary. As it turned out, you were more than capable
of taking care of yourself."

"I shouldn't have said half the things I did."

"In this case you should have. Otherwise she would have tried to chew you up and spit you out."

"At least Jeff tried to control her."

"Jeff shouldn't have put himself in that position, either. He's much smarter than that. He's really quite a complicated person. He's not the sort that most people like right away. Part of it is because he judges himself too harshly. He never feels he's done a good job. He can always find something he could have done another way that would have been better. But he's also one of those people who can't tell repartee from bitchiness.

"Yet you like him."

"Jeff has more quirks than a bedspring, but as a friend he's fiercely loyal. He's no fighter, but he once got into a brawl in junior high because some boys were saying things about me that he didn't like. He was beaten to a fare-thee-well, but he had stood up for what he believed in. Friendship is sacred to Jeff."

"I sensed a loyalty in him," she admitted. "But I'm an outsider. His friendship doesn't extend to me."

"In time it will, and then you'll see why I value him."

"What makes you think I'll be around that long?"

"I'd like for you to be."

Amaris was silent. She didn't know how much truth was in that statement. "I'm afraid to believe you."

"Why?"

"Because your words may not mean the same thing to you as they do to me. What do you consider a long time? Two weeks? Two years? Forever? We don't even talk the same language."

"I haven't drawn up a probability chart," he said in exasperation. "All I know is that you fascinate me. I want to spend time with you and get to know you better.''

"There's no reason for you to feel that way, I'm so ordinary. I've never been to Greece. I've never been out of the country at all! Do you know where my best vacation was spent? The Grand Ole Opry!''

"You're kidding,'' Blake said with a broad grin.

"See? I knew you'd laugh at me!''

"I'm not laughing. I'd like to go there someday myself.''

Amaris looked at him doubtfully. "I don't believe you.''

"Would you like for me to recite Waylon Jennings's latest hits? Sing a chorus from 'Blue Eyes Crying in the Rain?'''

"You listen to country-western?'' she exclaimed.

"Amaris, you only have one fault as far as I can tell. You're a snob.''

"What! Me?'' She stared up at him.

"Worse than that, you're a reverse snob. You aren't giving me a chance to be myself. You're too busy squeezing me into your preconceived idea of who you think I should be. I don't insult you by saying all waitresses do this or all waitresses do that. Can't you give me the same consideration?''

"A snob? Me?'' she repeated in a stunned voice.

"I don't hold it against you,'' he said with some amusement. "Some of my best friends are snobs. I just thought you should know.''

Amaris sat down on the wooden bench that joined the deck's railing. "Nobody has ever called me that before.''

"Sometimes it takes a good friend to tell you something like that." He sat down beside her and took her hand. "I'd like to be your friend."

She looked up at him with questioning eyes.

"And in time," he continued, "perhaps more."

Amaris didn't know what to say. She was rarely caught by surprise by any statement, but this time she was so taken aback by his suggestion that he thought their relationship could become deeper than friendship, she was unable to respond. Immediately she shifted her thoughts to his observation that she was being snobbish. As difficult as it was for her to accept this, she suspected he was right. She had less racial and religious prejudice than anyone she knew, but when it came to money that was another story. "I never knew I was a snob. I'll have to work on that."

"You're already pretty good at it," he teased.

"It's not funny! I'm supposed to know better."

"According to your beliefs, you get back what you put out. Right?"

"Yes. That's true. It's a bit more complex than that, but that's the essence. I didn't realize you were paying such close attention to the things I've said."

"I've listened carefully to every word and I agree with much of your philosophy."

"You amaze me."

"That gives us even more common ground for our friendship."

Amaris took his hand and measured hers against it, palm to palm. Deciding it was time to delve into the subject she had initially shied away from, she asked, "Do you really think we could continue being friends?"

"Unless you have some objection to it."

"What did you mean about being more than friends later?"

Blake put his arm around her and drew her head down to his shoulder. "You know what I meant."

His tone was unmistakable and she certainly did know. She'd even dreamed about becoming his lover. With Blake it would be so natural, almost as if it had been written in the stars. "Yes, I know what you mean."

"We'll take it as slowly as you like. I don't want you to rush into anything that you might regret."

"'The saddest words in human tongue, it might have.'"

"What?"

"You reminded me of a poem I learned in school. I'm not sure I said it exactly right, but that's close. I'm more apt to regret what didn't happen then what did." She smiled mischievously. "But we'll still take it slowly—for your sake."

Blake laughed heartily. "We do tend to attribute to others what we feel ourselves, don't we?"

"Were you hurt by Darla?"

He automatically started to deny it, then stopped. "Yes, I was." That really wasn't as true as he thought it should have been, but he didn't know why. Every time it occurred to him that he had been able to walk away from Darla with such ease, such detachment, he questioned whether he knew anything about love at all.

"It's understandable that you would feel that way. Most people are hurt when they lose a relationship."

"You see, it really came as such a surprise. We were at her parents' home in Atlanta and were supposed to make our engagement public that night, but instead she told me she'd fallen in love with someone else."

"You deserved better than that."

"I agree. But as I said before, that relationship is over for good. I seldom even think about her. Now you know why I was wearing a tux so early in the morning the day I lost my money clip. I'd driven straight back from Atlanta."

"I had wondered about that."

Blake looked down at her guileless face, bathed in the moonlight. What did he feel for this woman? It wasn't at all what he'd felt for Darla. Of course there were almost no similarities between them, but what did that have to do with love?

Maybe he wasn't through with Darla, he wondered. Maybe he was going through such strong denial he wasn't even aware of the pain he would have to endure when the denial phase of his grieving was over. When would he know? He couldn't bear the thought of doing anything that would hurt Amaris.

"Blake?"

"I'm sorry. What did you say?"

"You looked so far away. Is everything okay?"

"Sure," he said, pulling her close to him, hoping he hadn't told a lie.

Chapter Six

"I expected more from you," Blake said as Jeff Hancock settled into an armchair by the fire in Blake's den. "Last night was par for Karen, but you're supposed to be my friend. Why did you invite her?"

"It was actually her idea. She called me for the date. Several days later, she suggested we ask you to join us. I knew you'd want to bring a date, so I invited you to do that. If I'd been thinking, I'd have remembered how catty Karen can be—especially around women she's meeting for the first time. I don't know whether she feels threatened by them or what. But you've got to give me credit for trying to shut her up."

"I know you did. But with Karen that's like trying to stop a runaway train. Why do you date women like that? Can't you see how much she's like Andrea?"

"I don't know where you get that. Andrea is a short blond and Karen is a tall redhead. They aren't anything alike."

"Not physically maybe, but they're both sharks. If Amaris hadn't been so adept at taking care of herself, I would have told Karen what I think of her. And that would have been embarrassing for everyone."

Jeff sipped his scotch-and-water and said, "You can be sure that won't happen again. I'm through double-dating with Karen, although one on one she's a lot of fun."

Blake watched the fire leap and crackle on the grate. There was no use trying to get Jeff to change his taste in women. Blake could only hope his friend would eventually find someone kind to fall in love with. Someone like Amaris. "What did you think of her? Isn't she great?"

"Who?"

"Amaris, of course."

"She's a beauty, all right." The words were complimentary, but his tone was lackluster at best.

"Why do I get the feeling you're holding back?"

"Speaking as your campaign manager, she isn't right for you."

"You just said she's beautiful, and she's also intelligent. What more could she need?"

"A pedigree. And she says whatever pops into her head. I don't need to tell you that a quick tongue such as that could be suicide for a politician."

"Maybe I'm not cut out for politics."

"Bull. You were raised from the cradle to be at least a governor. Maybe even president."

"I don't want to date only women who can further my career. That's as bad as marrying for money."

Jeff was thoughtful for a minute. "That's occurred to me, too. Hasn't it dawned on you she may be after exactly that?"

"Don't be ridiculous."

"I could say don't be naive. Women have been known to date men for the fringe benefits."

"How did we ever get to be friends?" Blake intoned in a mock-threatening manner. "Half the time I don't even like you."

"All the same, you ought to pay attention to what I'm saying. You can't possibly have anything in common. You don't know the same people or go to the same places."

"So she hasn't been to Greece. So what? A lot of people haven't. That doesn't mean she wouldn't like to go or that she never will. Even if she doesn't, that won't mean anything, either."

"What if before we get you elected governor, some hotshot reporter gets hold of her? What if she makes some offhand remark about being half Indian?"

"It might get me the Indian vote."

"Or you might end up here at Eventide rather than in the governor's mansion."

"There are worse fates."

"Be serious, Blake. We're talking about not only your future but that of Virginia. A man like you could do so much for this state."

"Yes, I feel I could make a significant contribution. But did it ever occur to you that the voters might like to have a governor who is as real as they are?"

"No. Voters want a pretty package all tied up with a fancy ribbon. They want a predictable political machine. Up until you met this waitress, you fit the bill perfectly."

"Thanks," Blake said dryly. "Your compliments are underwhelming."

"You don't need compliments from me, you need a game plan. My job is to get you elected as governor of the Commonwealth of Virginia."

"And after that?"

"The U. S. Senate. Then we go for the big one."

At one time the idea of making it to the White House had been his ultimate goal, and with his family's connections and sterling record he stood a good chance of getting there. But now Blake no longer felt thrilled at the idea and was puzzled. "We've always had big plans, haven't we?"

"Damn right, and we're going to see them come to pass."

Blake stared at the fire and wondered.

LYLE DUNLAP'S VOICE shifted to a higher note as his anger flared through the phone lines. "Grace, I've put up with more from you than anyone else ever would have. I want to see the boys, and I want to see them today!"

Grace gripped the phone so tightly her knuckles ached. "We have other plans for today."

Todd came into the kitchen. "Is that Dad on the phone? Can I talk to him?"

"No. Go get ready."

Lyle's voice cracked with his rapidly growing rage. "I'm telling you, the boys better be there when I come over."

"Why can't I talk to him?" Todd complained.

"Your father says I can't take you boys to the movies," Grace snapped without covering the mouthpiece.

"I did not!" Lyle bellowed. "Put Todd on the phone!"

"No, I won't." Grace's face had gone chalky white with her fury. "I won't have you upsetting him."

"Me? You're the one lying to him!"

"Don't call me a liar!"

Todd's eyes widened.

Grace felt a stab of remorse as she saw tears welling in her son's eyes. "Todd, it's okay. It really is, honey." She reached out and hugged him. "Is Ben almost ready?"

Todd nodded sullenly and eased out of her embrace.

With a sigh, Grace turned away from him. Todd was all too much like Lyle. Thank goodness Ben had taken after her. "Lyle, I can't continue arguing with you. I don't have many afternoons off, and we have plans."

"Grace, I'm warning you. If you don't let me see the boys, I'm going to do something you'll regret."

Mental incompetence? "Don't you dare threaten me." As soon as the words had spewed unchecked from her mouth, she glanced around her, relieved to find she was alone in the kitchen. "You know you aren't man enough to follow through with your threats."

There was an ominous silence on the other end of the phone.

"Maybe you can bluff girls like Tiffany McNee, but I'm not buying it." Again she heard only silence. Grace felt suddenly uneasy. Lyle was never silent unless he was really furious.

"I'd like to keep discussing it," she continued with biting sarcasm, even though she knew she should have backed off, "but I have more important things to do." She listened closely for a response but heard only the faint rasp of his breathing. Then she hung up.

"GRACE? I DIDN'T EXPECT you today," Amaris said. "Come in." She smiled a welcome at Todd and Ben as she took their coats. "Would you boys like some cocoa? It's sure cold out there today." When they nodded, she went to the kitchen to get it for them.

The boys turned on her television and plopped down in front of it on the rug. Grace followed Amaris into the kitchen, her face long and her eyes puffy as if she'd been crying. As Amaris heated the milk, she asked Grace what was wrong, being careful to keep her voice low enough the boys couldn't hear her.

"It's Lyle again," Grace groaned. "Honestly, Amaris, he's making my life miserable."

"What now?"

"He insisted that I let him take the boys for a weekend, and when I told him no I think he threatened again to have me declared mentally incompetent!"

"Again? I thought he'd backed off from that. Even his own lawyer told him he didn't have a case. It sounds like an idle threat to me."

"But I've never known him to be so angry. I finally just hung up on him."

"Why don't I go over and talk to him? Surely there must be some way to work this out."

"No, I don't want to put you in the middle of all this."

"I don't mind."

"He's changed. I'm really afraid of him," Grace said. "It wouldn't be safe for you to get involved."

"Are we still taking about Lyle Dunlap? He would never hurt me."

Grace shook her head. "You don't know him as well as I do."

Amaris frowned as she stirred the cocoa into the warm milk. "I just find this all so hard to believe. Grace, I know it isn't easy, but you really need to try to see this whole thing in a larger sense. Try to see his point of view. Can't you give in a little? Just for the boys' sake?"

"How can you say something like that to me? Do you think I want to see them hurt?" Grace's face flamed scarlet and she looked away. "Lyle knows he can see the boys, if he comes to the house while I'm there."

"But, Grace—"

"Don't 'but, Grace' me. You've never had to live with him or anyone else. You've never been through a divorce!"

"No, but I know both of you, and I can't believe there is no way of smoothing this over a little." Amaris looked toward the boys to be sure they were listening to the television and not to the conversation in the kitchen.

"I don't want to smooth matters over with him."

"Look at Todd and Ben," Amaris pleaded in exasperation. "However you may feel about Lyle, they're trapped in the middle. How can you do this to them?"

"I can't believe you're talking to me like this! You're supposed to be my friend!"

Amaris put her hand on Grace's arm. "I *am* your friend. That's why I have to say this to you. The divorce has caused a war that's tearing the boys up. Can't you see that?"

"All I can see is you turning against me!"

"No, I'm not." Amaris poured the hot cocoa into two mugs and topped them off with some miniature marshmallows. After she carried the mugs to the boys, she went back to Grace and said, "Let's go into the back room where they can't overhear us."

Grace sat down at the table instead. "There's no need to do that. They're watching television and not paying any attention to us."

"Do you talk like this about Lyle where they can hear it?"

Grace shrugged. "They have a right to know what he's like."

"That's not right. Grace, can't you see this will eventually come between you and them? They won't turn against Lyle, they'll defend him."

Grace didn't answer.

"How about this for a solution: Lyle can visit the boys over here. That way you and he have some space, and the boys get to see their father."

"No."

"Then I could go over to your house, and they can visit while you're at work."

"I don't want Lyle in my house while I'm gone. I don't want him anywhere near my place."

"Then I could take the boys to his house."

"Absolutely not! You don't know what kind of orgies are going on over there!" The tears that had brimmed in Grace's eyes began to course down her cheeks. Her face was contorted with anguish; her pain was intense. But Amaris knew Grace well enough to feel certain she would rise above this bitterness in time.

"Grace, for goodness' sake," Amaris said with a laugh. "You know better than that."

"No, I don't. Besides, he may have a live-in girlfriend again, for all I know. You can bet he would never tell me if he did."

"You're divorced. He has a right to a life of his own."

"Not that kind of life in front of my sons!"

Amaris repressed a sigh and patted her friend's hand in a gesture of consolation. "So tell me about the threat he made. Just what did he say?"

"I don't remember, exactly. It wasn't anything specific. Just that he would make me sorry. But I know what he meant!"

"He might not have meant anything at all. He was probably angry, and just said the first thing that popped into his mind."

"He was angry, all right. I don't think I've ever known him to be quite that mad."

Amaris made a cup of coffee for Grace and brewed hot tea for herself. "Well? What do you plan to do?"

"I told the boys I'd take them to a movie. Do you want to go?"

"What's playing?"

"It's that movie about the motorcycles and the rookie cops."

"Haven't they seen that one?"

"Yes, but they wanted to see it again. Want to come along?"

"No, thanks. Once was more than enough for me."

"I'm hoping it will take their minds off this latest blowup with Lyle. Amaris, I really don't want to hurt them. I do mean all this for their own good."

"I know. I only think you need to look at it carefully. You may be creating problems for them that might not go away easily."

"I needed that."

"I don't want to hurt or alarm you. It's just that I can see it from a relatively unbiased point of view."

"As my friend, I had hoped you would be prejudiced in my favor." Grace stood up abruptly. "We have to be going. The movie will be starting soon and they hate to miss the beginning.''

"I'm sorry, Grace. I don't want you to be upset with me.''

Grace made no comment but went across the room and turned off the TV. "Boys, it's time to go.''

"Already?'' Ben complained. "Spider Man was just getting ready to spin his web.''

"We don't want to miss the beginning of the movie,'' Grace said with forced cheerfulness. "You can see Spider Man anytime.''

Todd got up and did as he was told but with silent resignation; Ben was still complaining as they left. As Amaris washed the cocoa and coffee mugs, she couldn't help but think of all the changes she'd seen in Grace. She had never before witnessed the aftermath of a bitter divorce up close like this, and it was enough to give her concern about marriage in general. Surely if Lyle and Grace hadn't been able to make it work, marriage must be difficult indeed.

When Blake popped into her mind, her brow furrowed. She and Blake had less in common than Grace and Lyle did, yet there were times in her reverie when Amaris was sure she could be happy with him. But then Grace must have felt the same way about Lyle. What happened to two lovers to turn them into enemies? Judging by the divorce rate, this was a common fate for an alarming number of couples.

All at once the house seemed too small and her world too confining. With her mind filled with doubt, Amaris called Blake and told him she needed to talk to him right away. She could tell he sensed the urgency in her voice and was glad he invited her over without asking for any details. In a matter of minutes she was on the road to Eventide.

This time at the gate to Blake's home, she was stopped by a uniformed guard. However, as quickly as the man heard her name, he swung the gates open to let her drive through.

Her second view of Eventide and its surroundings was as impressive as the first had been. The hues of autumn spread across the backdrop of mountains like a red-and-gold tapestry. The house itself was elegant and regal, as if the affairs of mortals could never mar its serenity.

At the door she was met by Blake. "No butler?" she asked.

"I saw you driving up."

With no preamble whatsoever, Amaris blurted out the question that was plaguing her. "Blake, why do people get divorces?"

A broad smile of amusement swept across his face as he escorted her in. Her spontaneity was one of her most endearing traits. But then he realized her question was sincere, and his expression became more serious. With a curious tilt to his head, he said, "I'm told it's almost always due to problems about money or sex."

"Too much, or not enough?" Amaris quickly pressed.

"I suppose it varies. Why are you asking?"

"I'm trying to understand my friend Grace. She and her husband, Lyle, were as happy as any couple I've seen, then all at once he ran off with a younger woman and he and Grace divorced."

"Than I would assume sex was the culprit."

"Now he's out of a job and not able to pay child support, so Grace won't let him see his children."

"I seem to remember you mentioning them before."

"I'm sure I must have. They've been on my mind a lot lately." She walked with him into the den. Though the room was spacious, the fire that burned brightly on the hearth made it cozy and inviting, and the view of the mountains from the large windows was spectacular. "I don't ever want to be in Grace's place," she continued.

"No one in his right mind ever plans to marry and then get divorced. It just happens."

"It really frightens me, though," she earnestly said, as she drifted toward the window. "Especially seeing so much bitterness between two nice people. At times I feel like I'm being fought over for custody of my friendship, even though I've seldom seen Lyle since they separated. If I feel this way, what must Todd and Ben be feeling."

"They are the children?"

She nodded. "Both boys have become sullen and they argue more than they did before. Grace doesn't keep her feelings about their father from them, and I made the mistake of telling her she should. Now she's mad at me."

"I guess she didn't want to hear your advice. Sometimes good friends can suggest things, with the best of intentions, that aren't received well."

"You're right about that. I hate to see them so unhappy."

Blake came to her at the windows and put his arm around her shoulder. "All marriages don't end in divorce. And sometimes the divorce is healthier than the marriage was."

"I don't understand."

"Wouldn't it be worst for the boys if Lyle were still in the house and they heard this battle waged constantly?"

Reluctantly Amaris nodded.

"Grace may still be grieving the loss. I suspect that in time matters will improve."

Amaris put her arm around his waist. "I'm glad you're my friend. I needed to talk to somebody."

"I'm glad I was here for you. I want you always to feel free to talk with me about things that are important to you."

"There you go using that word 'always' again."

"'Always' isn't usually considered to be an inappropriate word."

"I'll bet Lyle said he would always be there for Grace, too."

"He may have thought he would be. But even though you've said he left her for someone else, he may have had reasons you don't know about. Has he confided in you?"

"No, he hasn't. Grace and I were always closer. I'm sure he would feel awkward talking to me about it. It just worries me that it came as such a surprise—even to Grace."

"I don't think the breakup of any relationship is solely because of just one party."

Amaris wanted to ask him if he shared the responsibility for his fiancée breaking their engagement so unexpectedly but felt she would be prying into his private business and worried that he might be offended. Forcing a smile, Amaris said, "I suppose I get too wrapped up in my friends' problems. I always have."

"Speaking of friends, Jeff was here earlier and he apologized for last night."

"That's nice, but I don't think he likes me."

"What Jeff may or may not think about the women I date has no bearing on me."

Amaris pulled away and went to stand by the fire. She had hoped he would say her impression about Jeff not liking her was wrong. "What does he have against me? He doesn't even know me."

"It's nothing personal. Jeff's full attention is on the governor's race. He's my campaign manager."

"So you told me."

"Jeff takes his job quite seriously. Too much so at times."

"He's right, you know. I'm not a good choice for you to date. And don't tell me I'm being a snob. Jeff obviously agrees with me."

"But I don't agree with either of you."

Amaris shook her head in consternation. "Life can be so complicated."

"I want to continue seeing you."

"I want to be with you, too." Amaris's gaze was fixed on him as he came to her. "You mean so much to me. Today when Grace and I disagreed, you were the one I wanted to talk to."

"Do you think you will be able to patch things up with Grace?"

"Yes, this isn't the first time we've had an argument. Our friendship is stronger than that."

Blake acknowledged a discreet knock at the door. It was Spenser with steaming cups of mulled cider on a silver tray. When the butler left, Blake said, "Do you drink cider? I remember you don't like coffee."

"I love cider. Especially when there's a fire in the fireplace and it's chilly outside." She took one of the cups and tasted the steamy brew. "Wonderful!"

"It's one of my cook's specialties. This and a chocolate cake that oozes calories."

"Chocolate has always been one of my weaknesses."

"You'd never know it to look at you."

"I come from a slim family. I guess we have high metabolism."

"You've never mentioned your parents. Are they still in Chinquapin?"

"No, they died in an accident a few years back. I have some cousins but no close family. How about you?"

"My parents retired to Switzerland. They always loved it there, so they decided to move permanently. I see them every year or so."

"What do you think they would say about your dating me?"

"Dad says you sound interesting and Mom says you remind her of one of her sisters."

"I do?"

He nodded. "I write them pretty often. Mom is a dyed-in-the-wool correspondent. She writes volumes to everyone. Naturally I told them we had met."

"Why?"

Blake smiled and leaned over to stoke the fire. "Because I wanted them to know about you."

Amaris went to the plump navy couch and sat down. "My parents would have liked you. Blake, what's it like to summer in Greece?"

"The people are friendly and the climate is warm. It's a beautiful place."

"But what is it like to *do* it? To just pack up and go over there for a couple of months?"

"It feels free. I've always enjoyed traveling. In some ways people are the same all over the world and in other ways they're very different. I'm a dedicated people-watcher."

"So am I. That's what I like about working in the café."

"And I like the scenery in different places. You'd enjoy Switzerland, I'll bet, and England."

"I'd love to see them someday."

"Do you enjoy flying?"

"Sure."

Blake's smile broadened and he came to sit beside her on the couch. "We could fly over sometime."

"I couldn't afford that."

"I'll buy your ticket."

"No way." She put her mug on the coffee table as she shook her head. "I'm not dating you for your money."

"I know that. Are you going to limit our dates to picnics and maybe an occasional movie or restaurant?"

"Now you're making fun of me."

"No, I'm not. I'm only pointing out that there are more exciting things to do than to stay in Roanoke or Chinquapin."

"You're right about that."

"And since I can afford them, there's no reason not to enjoy them."

"There's faulty reasoning in there somewhere. I'm not quite able to put my finger on it, however."

"Think about it. I wasn't suggesting we jump on the plane this afternoon. Just consider it."

Amaris's lips tilted upward in a smile. "I'll think about it, but I'm not making any promises."

"Fair enough. In the meantime, I'd like to invite you to a party I'm having next weekend. If the weather holds we'll have it on the lawn, otherwise we'll bring it inside."

"I love parties. Of course I'll come."

"It's not all play, I'm afraid. Most of the guests have been invited for political reasons. Former Governor Creighton and his wife will be here. A couple of state senators, one of our state representatives and the mayor. I'll be asking the governor, who backed my opponent in the primary, to swing his support to me for the upcoming election. It's a bid for party unity."

Amaris looked stunned. "All those people and me? I won't fit in with them. I know almost nothing about politics."

"There'll be others who are not politicians. You'll like most of them. Representative Jimerson can be a bit pedantic, though, until you get to know him, but his wife is fun."

"How dressy will this be? I've never been to a party like this before." The question, for her, was rhetorical, as she had already mentally gone through everything in her closet and knew she had nothing appropriate, regardless of his answer. She certainly couldn't wear the same outfit she had worn on their last date.

"It's not formal. Just suit and tie for the men."

She wished that helped but knew it didn't. "Oh, I see." It occurred to her that now that she wasn't working at the café every day, she'd have time to make a new dress. Grace was good about knowing what was in style, and Amaris knew she could count on her help. "Are you sure it's a good idea to invite me to this?"

"I'm positive. This party will be the perfect way for you to meet some of those people who have been taking up so much of the time I'd rather have been spending with you."

"Did Jeff know you were going to invite me to this party?"

"I don't consult Jeff about everything I do." Blake smiled with confidence. "Jeff works for me, not the other way around. He's my campaign manager and my friend—he's not my keeper."

"I thought politicians cared about other people's opinions of them and their actions."

"I do, but I don't let it rule my life. I make my own decisions."

Amaris admired his strength of conviction, but she wasn't sure he was right about this. He was on the rebound from his broken engagement with Darla and might not be exercising good judgment about any of this. She cared a great deal for this man and didn't want to do anything to hurt him personally or politically. She almost turned down the invitation flat but reconsidered. "It's important to me for you to know my feelings won't be hurt if you decide, after thinking about things for a few days, that it would be better for me not to attend this party. Do you understand what I'm saying?"

"Of course I do. But thinking about it won't alter my decision."

"Will you promise me you'll think about it anyway?"

"Since it seems important to you, I promise."

Chapter Seven

"I wish you were going with me," Amaris said as she fidgeted in her chair.

"Be still before all your hair comes down again," Grace scolded. "You squirm worse than Ben."

Amaris forced herself to sit still while Grace smoothed her hair into a sleek chignon. The day after Blake had invited her to his gala party, he called to tell her he'd given his invitation careful thought and had not changed his mind. On one hand Amaris was relieved, but she also had her own reservations. However in the final analysis Blake was the politician, and if he wasn't worried about his relationship with her hurting his career, she shouldn't be worried either. "Do you think my hair will stay up?"

"It will unless you stand on your head. I've put enough pins in to keep it in place under normal conditions."

"What about my makeup?"

"You look perfect."

Amaris stood and went to the bed to finish dressing. As she had predicted, her friendship with Grace had weathered the argument they'd had, and in the past few days she and Grace had scoured fashion magazines and pattern books in search of just the right dress for her to wear to Blake's party. They had settled on a flame red dress in a soft wool blend, simple in styling and belted at the waist. Grace had helped lay out and cut the material, but Amaris had done all the sewing. From another pattern, Amaris had made a Chanel-type jacket in navy with a floral design of flame red and rose to be worn over the dress. As Amaris was a skilled seamstress, the ensemble was beautifully made.

"It's too dressy," Amaris fretted. "Blake said the party is casual."

"He also said suit and tie. It's not too dressy." Grace got a box from her purse and handed it to Amaris. "Wear this with it."

When Amaris opened the box, her eyes widened. "Your grandmother's necklace!" She held the art deco jewelry up to the light, marveling at its beauty.

The necklace's blood red stones were clasped in gold filigree. The workmanship was intricate, and while it wasn't an expensive necklace, the age of the piece made it special.

"I can't borrow it," Amaris protested. "What if I lose it?"

"You won't lose it. There's a strong clasp on it, and besides, you never lose anything."

"But still . . ."

"It will be perfect." Grace put it around Amaris's neck and fastened the clasp. After stepping back and viewing it critically, she smiled. "Perfect. Look in the mirror."

Amaris went to her cheval glass and nodded. In her mind's eye, Amaris could see Grace's grandmother the day the necklace was given to her. It was a twenty-fifth wedding-anniversary gift from her husband, and she was still deeply in love with him. Although Amaris wasn't sure, she felt Grace and her grandmother had a great deal in common. If so, Grace stood a good chance of repeating that kind of long-term happiness, if she was able to reconcile things with Lyle one way or the other. Amaris made a mental note to bring this up with Grace at a more appropriate time. Looking back at Grace, she said, "It really is just the right touch. Are you sure, Grace? You know how I feel about borrowing things."

"I know, and I'm overruling you. The necklace is going to the party with you, if I have to glue it on."

Amaris smiled. "Thank you, Grace. I'll be very careful with it."

"I'm not worried."

Going to her closet, Amaris slipped on her navy leather shoes and got down the matching purse from a high shelf. As she switched the contents from her everyday bag to the leather purse, her fingers fumbled over the familiar articles. "What if I say the wrong thing? I told you who all will be there."

"Just think before you speak. Everything will be okay."

Amaris zipped her purse and sat back down on the bed to relieve the wobble in her knees. Looking up at Grace, she said, "I'm so nervous I feel sick."

"There's no reason to be. It's a party, not a hanging. Blake is the host. What could be simpler?"

"A party without a former governor, the mayor of Roanoke and assorted senators and representatives?" she suggested.

"They may not even show up. If they do, you probably won't meet them. This sounds like a huge party and I'll bet you don't catch so much as a glimpse of them."

"I'm not that optimistic. What if I spill something all over the governor?"

"Simply say you're sorry, don't tell him your name and run like hell," Grace suggested cheerfully.

"Thanks. You really know how to bolster a person's confidence."

Grace laughed. "Quit worrying. Now get in your car and drive away, or you'll be late."

Amaris stood up and examined her reflection again. "Are you sure I'm not overdressed?"

"Get going, or I'll drive you there myself."

With a wavering smile, Amaris picked up her purse and let Grace escort her from the house. The afternoon was cool but pleasant, with a brilliant blue sky overhead. The day, Amaris concluded, was a spectacular one for an outdoor party and everything was nearly perfect—except for the intimidating guest list.

Amaris waved goodbye as she and Grace got into their respective cars. All the way to Eventide she felt increasingly nervous. After she was waved through the gates she realized she was dressed appropriately, but her car stood out from the others there like a lemon in a bowl of cherries. She parked as far away from the Mercedes and Cadillacs and Bentleys as she could. She couldn't recall ever having seen so many limousines gathered in one place.

The side lawn had been converted into an enormous outdoor room. Huge tents of red-and-white striped awning had been set up to shelter guests from the sun and wind, and their open sides did nothing to obstruct the view. As she stepped in she passed two flowing fountains, one featuring a brace of hunting dogs "splashing" through the water, the other a mermaid with water pouring from a conch shell. Beneath the central tent was a tabletop fountain of a different type, whose tiers poured champagne, Chablis and burgundy into separate basins. Some of the waiters in crisp white uniforms stood expectantly behind the tables, which had been laden with finger foods of all types, while others came and went with silver trays of wine-glasses. The garden's flowers were gone for the season, but what looked like hundreds of pots of flowers had been put in their place beneath the verdant shrubbery that defined the various garden areas of the lawn.

Amaris didn't see a single familiar face in the growing crowd, not that she had expected she would know anyone there other than Blake, but she had rarely been to a party where she was a complete stranger. She felt like a gate-crasher, especially since the other guests all seemed to know one another. Just when she was starting to feel lost and panicky, she saw Blake.

He grinned when he met her eyes and promptly came toward her. She was struck with how perfectly he fit into these elegant surroundings. He seemed as comfortable and at home here as he had on their informal picnic. But then he *was* at home. Amaris looked up at the rose-hued bricks of Eventide, and it occurred to her she didn't even know what all the rooms would be used for in a house like this. How could she possibly hope to fit into his world?

"I'm glad you're here," he said when he reached her side. "I had just gone inside to call you."

"I got behind every slow car on the road between here and there. Am I too late?"

"You're perfect."

His words implied more than her punctuality, and Amaris felt a wash of pleasure. "Thank you. You look very handsome."

"I was about to say how beautiful you look. You should wear red more often."

"I like bright colors. And I love the way you've decorated your lawn. I never expected striped awnings and silver. It's like a fairy-tale world."

"Some of us never entirely grow up," he said with a smile. "As a boy I always liked outside parties the best. If I could fit everyone into a tree house, I'd like that even better."

"You had a tree house? Here?"

"Of course. It was in that clump of trees you can see past the barn roof. I had hoped to hand it down to my kids someday, but a storm took it apart a few years back."

"You can rebuild it when you need it. The trees are still there."

"Yes," he said as he gave her a thoughtful look. "I plan to do that."

"I had a tree house, too," she reminisced happily. "Some friends and I built it in a tree that hung out over the creek that runs through town. It was so low over the water we could drop down and swim on summer days."

"Sounds great."

"It was. I had a happy childhood." She looked up at him. "Did you?"

"Yes, I did. There were always ponies and dogs and cats to play with, as well as lots of children. My parents loved to entertain, and most of their friends had children about my age."

"So you weren't a poor little rich boy? You weren't abandoned by your parents to a gin-swigging nanny?"

"Of course not," he said with a laugh. "You've seen too many movies. My parents and I are very close. I went on all their vacations and never once missed the joys of being born poor."

"Touché." She smiled up at him as he handed her a glass of wine from a passing waiter's tray and lifted his own glass in a toast.

"To us and a long friendship."

She raised her glass, then sipped the fruity wine. "Good. You have exquisite taste in wine."

"Thank you." His eyes searched the crowd. "Come with me. There's someone I want you to meet."

Amaris threaded through the crowd with Blake to where a tall man with silver hair was talking to a woman wearing a diamond necklace. "Ed, Bertie, this is Amaris Channing, the woman I was telling you about earlier. Amaris, this is Bertie and Ed Matthews. Ed is one of our state senators."

Amaris felt the ground weave under her as the man held out his palm to shake her hand. "I'm . . . I'm glad to meet you."

"Blake tells me you met only recently," the woman said. "I guess that's why we haven't seen you here before."

"Yes," Amaris said, then added, "Yes, we met recently." She tried to remember to weigh each word so she wouldn't make any embarrassing mistakes.

"Are you from Roanoke?" Ed asked.

Amaris shook her head. "I live in Chinquapin. It's not very far from here."

"Sure, I know where it is." Ed beamed as if the town were as familiar to him as his own backyard. "It has a creek that curves around through the town and there's a craft fair there each summer. July, I think."

"That's right," Amaris said in amazement. "You really do know where it is!"

"There probably aren't many places in Virginia that I don't know about," Ed said.

"Before he ran for the senate, Ed had a job overseeing tourism that took him all over Virginia," Bertie commented. "He still has to do a lot of traveling, but now I can go with him—all our children are grown and I have nothing keeping me at home."

"How many children do you have?" Amaris asked.

"Six. One from my first marriage, three from our own and two adopted. They really used to keep us busy," Bertie said with a laugh, as if the memories were full of pleasure.

Amaris began to relax. This down-to-earth woman was so easy to talk with she could have been one of the matrons from Chinquapin. "I've always wanted a big family."

"They're a lot of work and worry, but they're worth it. I tell Ed that every gray hair on our heads came from teaching our youngest daughter to drive. She could never remember which was the clutch and which was the brake. I was never so glad to see a child get her license as I was that one."

Amaris laughed. "I taught one of my cousins to drive and we nearly straightened out these mountain roads before she got the hang of it."

"How did you two meet?" Bertie asked. "Blake never told us."

Amaris's smile wavered. "I...I found his money clip and returned it." She might find Bertie easy to talk with, but that could be because Bertie and Ed didn't know who she was.

Blake put his arm around Amaris's waist. "I left it at the café where she works, and she tracked me down to return it. I had almost resigned myself to never seeing it again."

"You work at a café?" Ed asked.

If there was condescension in his voice, she couldn't detect it. She wished she had thought to read him when they shook hands, so she would know exactly how he felt about this revelation. She tried to pick up something from his thoughts, but her nervousness was blocking her efforts. Drawing a deep breath Amaris nodded. "Yes, the Mountain View Café."

Bertie smiled in commiseration. "I worked in one while I was putting myself through college. Those sure were long hours. Don't your feet hurt at the end of the day? Mine did!"

Amaris knew her mouth had opened in surprise, but she recovered quickly. "The small of my back is the problem." She glance at Blake, who was smiling smugly. He had apparently known all along that Bertie's background was similar to her own.

However, the illusion of similarity between them was shortlived as Bertie added, "And I had to learn colloquial French. I never got any of the orders right."

"French?"

"The café was in Paris. My parents sent me there to attend college, but I quit after my sophomore year. They ordered me to come home, and when I refused they cut off my allowance. That's when I decided to work in the café. It wasn't long before I realized I had made a mistake by quitting school, but my parents wouldn't agree to resume my support unless I returned to the States and transferred to Bryn Mawr, which was their first choice all along. But being the stubborn, rebellious young woman I was, I chose to stay in Paris, and after I had saved enough money I reenrolled in school and dropped back to part-time work. It wasn't easy, but I managed to work my way through."

"Oh." Amaris couldn't think of anything else to say. To her, Bryn Mawr, with it's ivy-covered walls and gobs of exclusivity, wouldn't have been a bad choice either.

"Did you go to school here in the States?" Bertie asked.

"Yes, I went to the University of Virginia."

"A great school," Ed put in. "Our oldest boy went there one summer."

Amaris knew the senator and his wife didn't intend for their words to be a put-down, but she saw a social chasm yawning between them. She and the senator's wife had no real common ground, and conversation beyond this point was going to be difficult.

Fortunately Blake must have sensed her discomfort, because he said, "If you'll excuse us, I see someone we need to speak to before he gets away." As soon as they were out of earshot, he asked, "What's wrong?"

"Nothing. Everything. Blake, I don't belong here."

"What are you talking about? Bertie was a waitress and one of their sons went to your college."

She shook her head. "If you don't see the difference, I can't explain it."

"You're being that four-letter word again."

"A snob?"

"You got it."

Amaris frowned up at him. "No, I'm not. But I am uncomfortable and you're being pigheaded."

Before Blake could argue the point, they were joined by Jeff Hancock.

"Jeff," Blake said, "I didn't see you arrive."

"I just got here. Hello, Amanda."

"Amaris," she corrected. She was fairly certain Jeff had remembered her name and had intentionally misstated it to put her off balance—or was she becoming paranoid? She wished she could gracefully leave.

Blake said, "I really do need to catch someone before he leaves. Jeff, will you keep Amaris company until I come back?"

"Sure," Jeff readily agreed.

Amaris watched Jeff's smile recede as Blake walked away. "It's a nice party, isn't it," she said in an attempt at small talk.

"Blake always throws a good party, and with all the right people." He looked squarely at her. "Did he mention the purpose of this gathering?"

"Yes. He said he's asking these people to support his candidacy for governor."

She didn't have to read Jeff's mind to know he hadn't changed his opinion of her. He obviously felt the last person Blake needed by his side on an occasion like this was a waitress from Chinquapin.

"So," Jeff continued, "your presence is quite a ... surprise ... to the rest of the campaign staff and myself. You see, we have a contingent from the press here." Jeff nodded toward several men and women who were grouped slightly apart from the others. "Once they figure out you're here as Blake's date, they'll be asking you for an interview, even though they've been instructed not to question any of the guests. Their only purpose in being here is to cover Blake's speech."

Amaris's eyes widened. "An interview? Me?"

"As one of Blake's good friends to another, I would advise you to avoid speaking with them." Although Jeff was smiling again, Amaris was sure his pleasant expression didn't reflect his true feelings.

"Are you concerned I will say something I shouldn't?"

"I don't know what you might say, but my job is to see to it that Blake's campaign is run smoothly and successfully."

"And you don't think I care about his future?"

"If you did, you wouldn't be here."

"Blake asked me to come," Amaris protested. "If he had thought my being here would be bad for him, he wouldn't have invited me."

"I'm not sure he gave the matter thorough consideration." Seeing that several of the reporters were looking their way, he took her arm and led her toward the mermaid fountain. "You see, Miss Channing, Blake lives in the proverbial goldfish bowl. Since the day this campaign began, everything he's said and done or will say and do is carefully weighed and discussed among the press. That includes his circle of friends."

"I can't believe this! He's not a royal prince!"

"For the next few years he may as well be. After he becomes governor we plan to aim for the U.S. Senate. Then the White House."

Amaris thought of Blake's key chain with its enigmatic M.P.—Mr. President.

"So you can see we have to be very discreet."

"Are you suggesting I should pretend not to be Blake's friend? Or that I should lie about it? I assure you I'm not a liar and will tell the truth if I'm asked."

"Then as his friend, please help him succeed by... backing away from this relationship with him—at least until he's elected governor. Do this for him."

Her eyes, as cold and clear as ice, bore into the man. She dared not speak. After a moment he drew back, and she briskly walked away toward the house. She had no idea where she was going, but she had to get out of the garden.

At the door a uniformed waiter met her and discreetly said, "Up these stairs and to the right, ma'am."

She followed his directions purposefully, as if the powder room had been her destination all along. At the top of the stairs, however, she turned left. The last thing she wanted was to confront any more of these people. She needed time to regroup and get her emotions under control.

The first door she came to was unlocked. After peeking inside to be sure she would be alone, she stepped inside and closed the door behind her, pressed the lock button and gratefully leaned against the door.

She found herself in a long room which was a combination bedroom and sitting room, obviously the one belonging to Blake.

She felt odd being alone in such a personal room, but the alternative was to go back downstairs and she couldn't do that until she'd had some time alone to think. Blake's campaign manager clearly felt her relationship with Blake would jeopardize Blake's political future. The same thought had already occurred to her and she found that disturbing. Blake had said he'd considered the impact and still wanted her there by his side. But if he was wrong and Jeff was right, Blake might, at some future time, resent her for costing him the election.

While trying to reason this out, Amaris began wandering through the spacious room. She didn't intend to pry, but she couldn't avoid looking at his belongings. Amaris padded over the silver-blue carpet to the double oak bookcase that met in the corner. As she read the titles of the books shelved there, she discovered two facts about Blake: he was more widely read than she had expected and it appeared he was indeed a lawyer. Somehow she had assumed his profession was simply millionaire. Most of the books had the well-read look of books which were as familiar as friends. Some of them were old favorites of hers.

Two comfortable armchairs were grouped with matching ottomans in the book corner. On the far end of the room was a large four-poster bed covered with a luxurious blue spread that matched the chairs. On the opposite wall was the fireplace, flanked by two matching armoires of impressive size. Because the house was over a hundred years old, it had been built with no closets, but a large walk-in closet had been fashioned from what must have originally been an adjoining servant's room. Like its owner, the room was well-organized and elegant.

Amaris gazed at the wide bed and ran her fingers over the heavy fabric of the spread. Blake slept here, lived here, came here for times of retreat. His imprint was on every object and in the air itself. To be in this room was to be in Blake's embrace. Amaris drew in a deep breath and let her senses revel in his memory traces.

Slowly she wandered over to the window that overlooked the back lawn, with its informal gardens and cobbled path that led down to the pristine barn. At first she thought the barn might be there for decoration only, but then she noticed several horses grazing in the paddock adjacent to the barn. Beyond was the grove of trees where Blake said he'd had his tree house. Here in his room, Amaris finally felt herself understand Blake.

He was complex but honest. His closest friendships were held back until he knew the person could be trusted, because there was a touching vulnerability beneath his polished exterior. His mind was quick and curious and he was a decisive man who was dedicated to helping others. In Blake's mind, this would be best accomplished as a leader of his country. Most flattering of all, Amaris found thoughts of her among his belongings. Especially on his bed.

She removed her fingers from the spread and straightened. Blake wasn't playing games with her. He really meant all he had said and implied. He cared for her as much as she cared for him. And regarding his career, he was ...

Suddenly her certainty about his feelings faltered and her thoughts were awash in a sea of ambiguity. Were her own thoughts and concerns becoming mixed with the intuitive perceptions she had been getting about Blake? Or was the ambivalence she was picking up a true reflection of Blake's feelings regarding the impact his friendship with her might have on his career? She wasn't sure which was true, but she did know that Blake was a decisive man and he had intentionally invited her to be here with him.

With her head high, Amaris left his bedroom and walked confidently back downstairs. Blake was a courageous man and she had enough courage to stand by his side. Enough to brave the formidable press and the prejudices that might have separated her from him. She hoped she was making the right decision.

Chapter Eight

lthough Amaris had gathered her courage, the scowl
at briefly darkened Jeff Hancock's face when he saw
er step out the side door of Eventide onto the lawn
reatened to bring back the quailing sensation Amaris
ad been fighting to overcome. Obviously he had as-
umed she had taken his implied suggestion that she
ave the party. Amaris defiantly raised her chin and
oked away from the man. She was an invited guest
nd was determined not to let anyone spoil this occa-
on for her.

A woman in the knot of the press correspondents
eparated herself from the others and edged toward
maris. The tag she was wearing clearly identified her
s one of the reporters. As Amaris smiled in greeting
t the woman's approach, she reminded herself to be
specially attuned to this stranger.

"Hello, I don't believe we've met," the woman said.
My name is Laura Irving. I'm with the Roanoke
ourier."

"I read your column regularly," Amaris said as she
nook hands with the woman, using the physical link
 help establish better mental contact. Instinctively she
new this was someone she could trust not to distort

the truth or use the facts to malign Blake. "I'm glad to meet you. I'm Amaris Channing." She could sense the woman's mental gears whirling in an effort to recall an influential family in the area with the last name of Channing.

"Of course," Laura said, though she clearly had no idea who Amaris was or why she was there. "Are you here with Jeff Hancock? I noticed you talking with him earlier. Perhaps you could give me some information about Mr. Hancock's plans as Blake Mayfield's campaign manager."

"I'm afraid I can't. And I'm not here with Mr. Hancock. My date is Blake Mayfield." The reporter's thoughts leapt with excitement, though her expression showed little change.

"You're with Mr. Mayfield? Then I do indeed want to talk to you."

"I'm afraid I don't have anything to tell you. Blake and I have only known each other for a short time."

Laura extracted a small tape recorder from her purse and was holding it between them so all of Amaris's words would be captured on tape. Amaris felt a twinge akin to stage fright. Out of the corner of her eye she saw Jeff wheel and stalk away, presumably in search of Blake.

"Are you from Roanoke, Ms. Channing?" Laura was asking.

"No, I live in Chinquapin. At the present I'm doing some writing and craft work. That's how I spend my winters."

"I see. You're an artist and writer?"

"Only during the winter. The rest of the time I work at the Mountain View Café." Amaris hoped she was doing the right thing in giving this interview. Being evasive about the truth would only create suspicion. Blake was determined to put her in the public's view, and she knew any reporter in the world could trace her to the café. The only way to handle what could be an awkward situation was to treat it as if it meant nothing at all.

"You're a restaurant owner? Is this a chain?"

"No, no," Amaris said with a rippling laugh. "I don't own it. I only work there. I'm a waitress."

Laura snapped the recorder off. "Are you serious? A waitress?"

"Would I lie to a tape recorder?"

Laura punched the machine back on. "I have to admire your honesty, Ms. Channing. How on earth did you meet Mr. Mayfield?"

"He left his money clip behind at the café and I returned it to him."

"Was there any money in the clip?"

"Yes, quite a bit in fact."

"And you returned it, too, I assume."

"Of course. It didn't belong to me." Amaris saw Blake approaching with his campaign manager hard on his heels. "Here comes Blake now."

The reporter's eyes nervously darted about, and Amaris sensed the woman's feelings of guilt. "We, the press, I mean, were invited to cover the speeches. I'm not supposed to be doing any interviews with the guests."

"Then I suggest you put away your recorder." Amaris returned Laura's grateful smile. At least one reporter would be on her side, she thought.

Blake smiled as he extended his hand to Laura, but his eyes were wary. "You're Laura Irving from the Roanoke *Courier,* aren't you?"

"Yes, sir. I believe we met at a fund-raising dinner for Senator Matthews last spring."

"Laura and I were just talking," Amaris said with an easy manner she hoped would allay any concern Blake might have. "I read her column every day."

Blake relaxed a bit. "So do I. You're an entertaining writer, Ms. Irving."

"Thank you. I'm flattered that you read my articles."

"However," Jeff said, "you were expressly forbidden to annoy our guests by asking for interviews. I'm afraid I must ask you to leave."

"What interview?" Amaris said innocently. "Were you interviewing me, Laura? I assumed we were talking about my Indian craft work."

"Yes," Laura picked up quickly, "we were talking about crafts. Could you tell me more about them?"

"If you would like to come to my house sometime, I could show them to you." Amaris's invitation was genuine and she hoped the woman would accept it as so. "I do weaving and bead work using the old designs and methods."

"You're Indian?" Laura asked.

"Partly. My mother was a full-blooded Cherokee."

Laura raised a curious eyebrow. "Amazing."

"Naturally none of this is public information," Jeff said, shooting a murderous look at Amaris. "Miss Channing is exaggerating and—"

"No, she isn't," Blake said, casting a warning glance toward Jeff. "I've seen a shawl she made and her work is magnificent."

Amaris smiled. She hadn't realized he had paid any attention to her wrap the night she took him out onto the deck in the moonlight. "Thank you, Blake. That's one of my favorite designs. It has to do with the legend of how the Milky Way was formed. The pattern is called *Gil' LiUtsun' Stanun'yi.*"

"You speak Cherokee?" Laura asked.

"Only a few words, I'm afraid. I'm happy to say there's a movement afoot to preserve the language, but not many people can still actually speak it."

"You never cease to amaze me," Blake said.

Amaris proudly smiled.

"I was wondering where you were," Blake continued. "I've been talking with Governor Creighton, and we were about to start the speeches."

She put her hand in his, a gesture noted by both Jeff and Laura. "I wouldn't miss this for anything."

Laura discreetly rejoined the other reporters, while Amaris walked with Blake and Jeff to the podium under the far canopy.

The former governor was the first to speak, and as his political rhetoric continued with no apparent end in sight, Amaris was glad she had not worn shoes with higher heels. Even so, her feet and legs were aching by the time the governor concluded his speech with the words, "And now, without further ado, I'd like to present a man we all know. A man who has not only hosted this fine party but the man to whom I'm giving my wholehearted support in his bid to be the next governor of the Commonwealth of Virginia. Ladies and gentlemen, Blake Mayfield."

Amaris applauded with all the others until her palms burned. As he stepped up onto the low platform, so handsome and charismatic, her eyes felt hot with unshed tears of admiration. He turned his boyish smile on his guests and Amaris saw every woman melt a little.

"I'm glad you could all come out to my get-together. If there's one thing my family has always enjoyed, it's having friends over." He waited for the chuckles to die down.

"My friend here," he said indicating the former governor, "has given me a big compliment in pledging his support to my campaign. As we all know, Virginia has seldom had a leader of his caliber. His capable shoes won't be easy to fill, but I promise all of you I'll do my best."

Amaris saw the reporters edging nearer, anxiously double-checking their tape recorders.

"At this time," Blake continued, "I would like to say that our party is now unified, and after I'm elected governor I will not only serve the will of those who have supported and elected me but the best interests of every citizen of Virginia."

The roar of approval all but drowned out Blake's last words. Jeff leaned near Amaris and muttered, "See how it is? It would be such a pity for this to be taken from him."

Amaris ignored Jeff and added her applause to that of the rest of the crowd. She had no intention of doing anything to disrupt Blake's political career. After all, she was a friend, not Blake's wife, and she didn't believe she would be a liability at all. If he wanted her by his side, that's where she would be.

After some additional remarks, Blake stepped down from the platform and the crowd closed in around him to shake his hand. His smile was wide and genuine as he made his way toward her through the throng. Taller than most of the people there, Blake was easily visible. She could scarcely believe that someone so heroic was interested in her. A niggling doubt suggested that perhaps her garden-variety roots were what interested him most, but she shoved the thought aside. She knew Blake wouldn't use her in order to secure the popular vote. If anything, she wondered if Blake shouldn't be listening to Jeff's advice about too close an association with someone from outside his own social stratum.

In only a moment he reached her side, and although he didn't introduce her to any of the reporters, they could all see she was with him. Amaris felt a wave of claustrophobia as the well-wishers and reporters closed around them. Crowds had always made her uneasy; they sent out such a mixture of thoughts and emotions that her sensitive nerves were always abraded. Now she discovered that a crowd with one exuberant emotion and one key thought was even more overwhelming. She touched her elbow to Blake's side for security.

ALTHOUGH THE REPORTERS left immediately after Blake's speech, his other guests lingered for another hour. Next to go were the politicians and their wives. But it was not until Jeff said goodbye, that Amaris breathed a sigh of relief.

"I really should go," she said as the last of the guests departed.

"Not yet."

"It'll be dark soon. You must have had a hard day. All those people to talk to and everyone watching your every move. Surely you must want to rest."

"Far from it. Parties like this get me so geared up I have trouble relaxing for hours after everyone is gone. Stay with me for a while. If you're nervous about driving home after dark, I'll follow you."

"All the way to Chinquapin? I wouldn't dream of asking you to do that. Besides, I'm not afraid to drive the mountain roads at night. I know them by heart."

"In that case, come inside. The sun will be down soon and the evenings are getting quite cool."

Arm in arm, they entered the house through the side door she had used earlier. "I love your house. It's like the ones I've seen pictures of in fine magazines—*Architectural Digest,* for instance."

"Actually, that magazine featured Eventide in one of its issues several years ago."

"Nothing on paper could do it justice." Amaris strolled to the wide windows of the side parlor and looked out at the softening sky. "This is the same view as from your den."

"Yes, the den, at one time known as the front parlor, adjoins this room. In the old days, after dinner the men would have adjourned to the den to smoke their pipes and cigars and discuss dogs or horses and their ladies would have congregated in here. Both groups would have a magnificent view of the sunset."

"You must love Eventide."

"Yes, I do. I'm like the mythical Greek giant who drew his strength by touching the land. Eventide revives me when the pace of life gets too hectic. I enjoy traveling, but I always enjoy coming home, too."

"I can see why." Amaris looked at him. "I have a confession to make. Earlier I felt I had to get away for a while, and I found myself in your bedroom. I hope you don't mind?"

"Not at all."

"I felt you in every corner and on every surface. I never understood you, until I stood alone in your room and let it talk to me."

"And now you do?"

"Yes, and I like what it told me."

"Which was?" He came to her and put his arms around her.

"You're one of the last genuine white knights. A Don Quixote, ready to attack any windmill that might be a giant."

"Somehow I imagined myself in a more prosaic light."

"Don Quixote was very brave," she said. "He had no idea those were only windmills."

"Are you saying my campaign is filled with useless causes?"

"No, just the opposite. I don't know what your platform is, but I know you have high ideals."

"My bedroom told you all this?"

"Psychometry comes in quite handy. If I hadn't gone in there by mistake, I probably would have slipped away before the speeches."

"Oh? Did something happen I don't know about? Was it Jeff?"

"It was nothing. Really. But for a few minutes I thought that my being there, my being too close to you, might hurt your campaign." Amaris stopped short of mentioning the ambivalence she had detected regarding his feelings on that issue.

"It was Jeff." Blake's brow creased in anger. "Just what did he say to you!"

"No, no. It wasn't important. Forget it. Jeff is a close friend, and I'm sure he's a very capable campaign manager. He has only your best interests in mind."

"Nobody has the right to say anything that makes you feel uncomfortable, and he sure has no right to come between us!"

"He hasn't done that. I'm still here, and it has occurred to me that I may be able to aid you with your campaign. I think I could help you understand what the ordinary people want and think. I hear it all day in the café."

"I certainly couldn't ask for a more beautiful political adviser."

She smiled and put her arms around his neck. "Thank you for the compliment."

Blake gazed down into her eyes and spoke with sincerity as he said, "From the first time we met, I knew you were special. When you returned my money clip and rushed away before we had a chance to talk, I knew I had to find you and get to know you."

"You never did say how you managed to find me."

"I had your license plate traced. Someone owed me a favor. If I had been unable to get the information that way, I would have gone back to the café."

"I'm flattered."

"I would have resorted to knocking on every door in Chinquapin if necessary."

"Do you always go to such lengths to get what you want?"

"If it is important to me, I do."

His voice was seductively low, almost mesmerizing, and she was sure the meaning of his words extended far beyond their discussion of his finding her address. Deep inside her Amaris felt the reawakening of an elemental need for Blake, much as she experienced every time they were alone together and close. As she gazed into his eyes, clear to the depths of his soul, the affirmation she sought came to her. Yes, this was a man she could love.

But then doubt crept in. Sometimes it was hard to tell whether she was intuiting things or whether it was her own wishful thinking. And she wasn't at all certain that he could love her or be able to commit himself to a long-term relationship with her, even if she wanted to. He had said he would go to great lengths to get what was important to him, and this surely implied that he would also make whatever sacrifices were necessary as well. The one thing that was abundantly clear was that he wanted to be the next governor of Virginia.

Without taking his eyes from hers, Blake drew a deep breath and said, "Amaris, I know we haven't known each other long, and I'm not sure if I ought to tell you this, but I . . . care a great deal for you."

Suddenly Amaris released the breath she hadn't realized she had been holding. For an instant as he paused she was sure he was going to tell her he loved her, but it was an unrealistic expectation. After all, as he had said, they hardly knew each other. Finally aware she hadn't responded, she said, "I care a lot for you, too."

"What do you think we ought to do about it?" His voice reverberated throughout her entire being. His eyes were a deep green, the same hue they had been the day of their picnic when he had first kissed her.

"I don't know," she admitted. "You aren't an average person—you stand every chance of being a leader of at least this state, and eventually our entire country. I want to continue seeing you, but I don't want to do anything that would hurt your political career, and I'm not so sure that you don't have some doubts about the wisdom of our dating."

"What have I said to give you that idea?" He released her and stepped back.

"It's not what you've said, it's that I sense an ambivalence within you."

Blake's eyes grew dark and he appeared somewhat aggravated. "Aren't you taking this psychic intuition a bit too far? Shouldn't my clear and unambiguous statement of how I feel about you outweigh your 'perception' of my inner thoughts?"

"Please don't be offended. I'm only trying to protect you."

"Jeff wants to protect me. You want to protect me. Doesn't anyone close to me trust my ability to decide what is best for me? Must I be protected from myself? I think not."

"But I—"

"If you want to talk about sensing others' true feelings, I would say that you are afraid of getting too close to me and you are using my career as an excuse."

For a long moment, Amaris didn't answer. Her immediate thought was to deny Blake's suggestion, but as she considered the misgivings she'd had, she realized there was a bit of underlying truth in what he had said.

"Blake, it isn't that I'm afraid of getting too close to you, but I find your life-style . . . intimidating."

"If you're going to bring up the money issue again—"

Amaris reached out and gently silenced Blake by putting her finger to his lips. "Blake, my privacy is important to me."

"Privacy is important to everybody."

"But you can accept having the press follow you about, reporting your every move on television and in the newspapers. I'm not sure I can live like that." She looked down, then turned away from him. "I've said too much. I didn't mean to imply this has to be permanent or that I expect you to propose to me or anything else. But I don't want you thinking that I am afraid of being close to you. If anything, the opposite is true."

Blake drew her back to face him and gathered her into his embrace. Resting his cheek on her sleek hair, he said, "I was wrong. I'll never accuse you of that again. I suppose I was afraid that it might be true and I had to know." Although Amaris didn't speak, he felt her nodding her understanding against his chest. "It's taken me a number of years to prepare myself for the concessions I knew I'd have to make to effectively compete in the political arena and it wasn't a decision I made lightly. I'm not asking you—"

Amaris abruptly pulled back from him, shaking her head. "There's too much at stake here for either of us to make a hasty decision about any sort of long-term commitment in our relationship."

Without another word Blake bent and brushed her lips with a tentative kiss, as if he were testing her willingness for more. She could see the growing passion in his eyes and had no doubt that he wanted to make love with her. She tilted her head so he could see the acceptance in her smile, then said, "Jeff won't be pleased at this turn of events."

"To hell with Jeff." He pulled her into his embrace and kissed her for a long time. When he drew back, he murmured. "A kiss like that could drive a man crazy. And you smell and taste better than anything on earth. There was no music until I met you."

"Every time you kiss me I see beautiful colors which have no names and I sense that we have known each other forever."

"Come upstairs with me. Stay with me, Amaris."

"For tonight," she whispered. "I can stay with you for tonight."

"And tomorrow?"

"Tomorrow, we'll see."

Arm in arm they matched their steps as they climbed the stairs. Blake's household staff was well trained to stay out of sight until needed, and Amaris felt as if the two of them were alone in the house.

"Eventide was built for a bride," Blake said as they crossed the upstairs foyer to the door to his bedroom. "Many of the houses of this vintage were. But this bride was unique. Her name was Maria Desirée Jacqueline Broussard, and she was Creole French. Her family disinherited for marrying an 'American'—meaning non-Creole. They threw her out and expected her to die of a broken heart."

"How sad. And did she?"

Blake laughed. "Not at all. She and her husband both lived well into their eighties and died surrounded by dozens of children, grandchildren and great-grandchildren. According to our family legend, they were so happy together, she never missed her estranged family at all."

"I like that legend."

"My grandmother said I look like her, since I have dark hair."

"I can easily imagine you as a Creole in New Orleans. You have an aristocratic air about you."

Blake closed his bedroom door behind them, locking it to ensure their privacy. Amaris walked to the windows on the far side of the room and gazed at the brilliant sunset. "That reminds me of the one thing I don't like about Chinquapin," she confessed. "It's in such a deep valley, we don't see sunrises or sunsets."

"You can come here and watch sunsets every night if you'd like."

Amaris smiled. "The sunsets aren't the only draw to Eventide. I'm afraid I'm far more interested in you than I am in the sunset."

Blake took her in his arms and kissed her. As Amaris's lips parted, he ran his tongue over the ridges of her teeth and she met his tongue with her own. Amaris had kissed other men, but she had never kissed anyone who was as masterful as Blake. He knew exactly how to hold her and how to move his lips upon hers to stir the depths of her soul.

Moving slowly, as if he had all the time in the world, his hand glided up her slender waist and onto her breast. After gently exploring her entire breast his fingers spiraled in to the center, and as he rubbed his thumb over her nipple Amaris felt as if all her senses would explode. She wanted him, and she wanted to make love with him all through the night.

He brushed the jacket off her shoulders and let it drop to the plush carpet. In her beautiful red dress, she stood like a flame against the cool colors in his room. As he watched, she lifted her arms and removed the pins from her hair and let the silken skein fall to her shoulders. Blake ran his fingers through her thick tresses and felt how warm her hair was from having been pinned close to her head. Her eyes were as dark as a stormy sky and her lips were slightly parted in invitation.

With his eyes on hers, he reached around her and eased down the zipper of her dress. The soft wool fell away at his touch and pooled at her feet. Amaris stepped out of her shoes as she moved free of the dress. She wore a garnet teddy of clinging satin and lace. Her legs were slender in the silken sheath of her hose. Blake thought he had never seen a more beautiful woman.

Amaris watched his face to see what he was thinking and feeling, rather than probing his mind. She had had little experience and was shy about being seen with so little on. However, Blake's admiring gaze reassured her.

She removed his suit coat, pulled free the knot in his tie and drew it from around his collar and let it drop upon her dress. One by one she opened the buttons of his shirt as he reached around her and unbuttoned his cuffs.

Blake's body was firm and his skin tone was a pale bronze. As he removed his shirt, she noted that his arms were strong but not beefy and hard muscles fanned across his chest and ridged his belly.

At the bed, Blake slipped the straps of the teddy over her shoulders and eased the filmy fabric down to her waist. Amaris's breasts lifted proudly and the excitement of his gaze beaded her nipples. Blake cupped a breast in each of his palms and traced lazy circles over her nipples with his thumbs. Amaris felt his touch reach all the way to the center of her being.

"You remind me of a song that was popular a few years ago," she said. "It was about a man with slow hands, a lover with an easy touch."

Blake smiled down at her. "I plan to please you again and again. I intend to make love with you, not merely go to bed with you."

Reaching past her, he pulled back the bed covers, exposing the pale blue sheets. He laid her down upon them, then skimmed the teddy and her hose over her hips and off her legs. As he studied her body, Blake finished undressing himself then lay down beside her.

At the first touch of his body against hers, Amaris drew in her breath. Every nerve in her body was sensitized to the warmth of his flesh. Rosy light from the sunset blushed their skin and romantically softened the room. His thick black hair fell over his forehead, and she saw the promises of loving in his eyes.

"You're so beautiful, I'm afraid you may vanish," he said at last. "I can hardly believe you're here and that you want me to make love with you."

"I was just thinking the same thing about you," she confessed. "You're so perfect. I feel like Cinderella with the prince."

"I'm not perfect. Far from it. But I enjoy your being here with me and want to make you happy."

"I'm already happy." She ran her hand over the hard wall of his chest and smiled.

"I'm glad I found you," Blake said, then covered her lips with his own and deeply kissed her.

As his hand stroked her hip and moved up to caress her breasts, her excitement grew. She felt as much one with him as it was possible for one human to feel for another. His touches thrilled her and she loved the way their bodies matched curve to curve and plane to plane.

Blake lowered his head and kissed a trail of fire down her neck and over her chest until his lips replaced his fingers on her breast. His tongue lathed her nipple and licked it to aching tenderness. Amaris moved beneath him in ecstasy and offered herself to his taste and touch.

His hand caressed the swell of her hip and drew her even closer against his body. When she felt the hot hardness of his manhood pressing against her, her pulse quickened. He wanted her as badly as she wanted him. There was no doubt about it.

Amaris had only been with one other man, and she felt a wave of doubt over whether she could please Blake. He was a skilled lover and he knew exactly how to kiss and caress her to make her want him even more. She wished she were more experienced, so she would know ways of giving him more pleasure. In lieu of experience, she let her intuition guide her.

Blake sighed with pleasure as she moved sensuously against him. "You feel so good," he said into her hair. "So damned good!"

Amaris looped her leg over his and rolled so that she lay beneath him. As he entered her, she raised her hips to welcome him. He slid into her moist warmth and held still for a moment as he fought for control. When he began to move, Amaris responded, matching her strokes to his.

As her passion rose, Amaris quickened her pace. A deep need replaced her wanting, and she moved with growing anticipation.

All at once the heat in her veins centered deep within her being, and she felt her culmination begin to build. As if Blake's senses were directly tied to her own, he also became more intense in his loving. When she could hold back no longer, Amaris released all her passion and reached the peak of her desire. Blake cried out softly and held her tightly as her pleasure triggered his own.

Together they rode the crest of love, then gently drifted into its afterglow. "You're perfect," Amari murmured; when her breathing had slowed to the point where she could speak. Her bones felt like jelly and her mind was still melded with his. "So perfect!"

"You inspire me." He moved to one side so that she was nestled comfortably in the protecting curve of his arm and as he stroked her hair, he said, "As a matter of fact, you're inspiring me again."

Amaris gave him a knowing smile. "I agree. We can sleep another time."

Blake tilted her chin up and kissed her with even more passion than ever.

Chapter Nine

"You're amazing," Blake said to Amaris as they left the school. "I know you must have given that speech many times before, but it sounded fresh and spontaneous. I know some politicians who could take lessons from you. What's your secret?"

"I never thought about it much. Maybe it's because I don't speak from notes." Amaris glanced around and to be sure no one else was in earshot, then added, "Or it could have been because of the exhilaration I still feel from last night."

Blake's face seemed to light up with the reminder of their first night of loving. "I'm glad you invited me to come here with you. I hated the idea of you having to leave so early this morning and us not being together."

"I'm flattered that you're interested in the things that interest me."

"As I said, I think what you're doing is important. And I'm proud to see you do it so well. Both you and the policewoman have a special knack for talking with children. You held their attention, even when you were speaking to their parents. And the children enjoyed being fingerprinted, too. That surprised me. The whole program was professionally delivered. I should fire Jeff and make you my campaign manager. You're efficient, well-organized and a hell of a lot prettier.''

''No, thanks. I don't want the job. I'm no politician.''

Blake opened the car door and helped her in. Before he shut it, he said, ''Do you really dislike politics as much as you seem to?''

Amaris was thoughtful as she considered her answer. ''I know politics are important. Goodness knows, we couldn't run the country without them. But I have a real problem with politicians who make campaign promises to win votes, then don't follow through—for whatever reason. Politicians seem to create this sense of their word being unreliable.''

''Does that mean you don't trust my word?''

''No, I believe you. But not all politicians are as trustworthy as you are.''

''How do you know I can be trusted? Is it because you've read my mind?''

''Partly. But I also have an intuitive sense that you're a man of your word. Does it bother you that I've read your mind?''

''It's a little unsettling that my thoughts are not as private as I believed, but I have nothing to hide.''

''If it helps, you should know that I don't have the ability to read all your thoughts, and in fact I feel I have an obligation not to try. I don't allow myself to idly eavesdrop.''

''I trusted you wouldn't,'' he said with assurance.

He closed the car door and came around to get in beside her. ''Which place in town has the best food? Mountain View Café?''

"Yes, but I'd rather not go there. I find it difficult to enjoy a meal in a place where when I'm used to taking the orders and busing the tables. Let's go to the Sugar Maple Restaurant."

As Amaris had said, the food was satisfying, though not excellent, but Blake was more interested in Amaris than the meal. The pale green sweater and bottle green slacks she'd changed into before going to the school were perfect colors for her, and her freshly shampooed hair was as glossy as a raven's wing. Thoughts of the shower they had shared at Eventide that morning after making love again in the light of dawn made Blake want her again.

"What are you thinking?" she asked.

"I was wondering if I'll ever get enough of you."

She smiled and blushed. "That's occurred to me, too," she admitted.

"How do you plan to spend your afternoon?"

"I have no plans," she said with a smile. "I have to return Grace's necklace, but after that I'm free."

"How would you like to go to my cabin with me? We'd only be able to stay overnight, though, since I've got to be in Charlottesville tomorrow afternoon, and then on to Alexandria for two days." When he saw her smile fade, he added, "I wish I didn't have to go, too, but it can't be helped. At least we'll have the night together, and I know you'll enjoy the view there. The cabin's on Long Hair Mountain. Isn't that an odd name? I've often wondered why it was named that."

Trying to cover her disappointment that his campaign would separate them again so soon, she forced herself to cheerfully respond to his last question. "I know the answer. Long Hair is one of the seven clans in the Cherokee tribe. My family is in the Deer clan."

Blake reached across and took her hand in his. "Please come to the cabin and stay the night with me."

Realizing how foolish she would be to turn down any time she could have with him simply because she wished it could be more, she said, "I'd love to go to your cabin with you. I'll just need to pack a few things."

"Pack light," he said with a seductive smile. "You won't need much."

Laughter lit her eyes as she put her hand over his. "Now I know I'm looking forward to it."

She glanced up as two women entered the restaurant. The younger of the two gave Blake an appraising look that bordered on being flirtatious. Amaris looked away. "That's Tiffany McNee. She's the one Lyle left Grace for. I thought she'd moved to Richmond."

Blake followed her glance and found the woman still staring at him. "She seems pretty obvious to me."

"I believe that's what attracted Lyle."

Later, as Blake paid their check at the cash register, Amaris noticed Tiffany's come-hither stare toward Blake. Tiffany was so busy trying to make eye contact with Blake, she wasn't aware that Amaris was watching her.

Until now, Amaris had had some difficulty with Grace's animosity toward Tiffany because she had assumed Lyle must have first given the girl some indication he was interested in her. But clearly Tiffany needed no invitation to flirt and wasn't the least bit subtle.

"That girl is a predator," Amaris commented to Blake as they drove away. "Lyle and Grace were having problems, and Tiffany stepped in at just the right moment when Lyle was vulnerable and distracted him from trying to work things out with Grace. Once the divorce was final, she dumped him. It seems as if she did that just to see if she could break them up. I'll bet she doesn't even know what love is."

"Who does?"

Amaris started to respond that *she* did, but couldn't get the words out because of the curiosity his statement had aroused in her. Did Blake not know about love? She couldn't reconcile how someone who was so skillful at lovemaking could be so closed off from his feelings as not to know what it felt like to love someone else. But, then, he had been engaged to be married and seemed to have given up his fiancée a bit too easily.

Quickly she chided herself for judging anyone else's perception of what love between a man and a woman was supposed to feel like. To her it meant a sense of commitment and some sort of indefinable bonding of souls. But maybe it was different for others. Maybe that was why so many married people who professed to love one another ultimately divorced.

Amaris remained wrapped in the silence of her own thoughts until they reached her house. After retrieving Grace's necklace, she gave Blake directions to Grace's house and they were off.

"What a surprise," Grace said as she greeted them at the door and showed them into the living room. "I've heard so much about you, Mr. Mayfield."

"Please, call me Blake," he said with a smile. "Amaris has told me quite a bit about you, too."

"Only believe the good parts," Grace said.

"Here's your necklace. Thanks for loaning it to me."

"I was glad to do it. Was there a good turnout at the party?"

Amaris sat beside Blake on the couch. "I think half the state was there. Former Governor Creighton announced he was moving his support to Blake and encouraged all his followers to do so as well. He said he was sure Blake would become Virginia's next governor."

Grace smiled nervously. "I never met a celebrity before. If I had known you were coming, I would have fixed myself up."

"You look fine," Amaris assured her. "I should have called, but we were already on our way here before I remembered."

Todd and Ben passed through on the way to the backyard, and Grace called them in to meet Blake. "He may be our next governor," she added as she finished the introductions.

"Can you play football?" Ben asked.

"Sure I can. I played on the team at college."

"Would you throw us some passes?" Todd asked. "Dad is teaching us, but we don't get to practice very often." He cast an accusing look at his mother.

"Todd, don't bother Mr. Mayfield with that," Grace protested with an apologetic glance at Blake.

"It's no bother at all. I'd enjoy it." Blake winked at Amaris before letting the boys lead him away.

"He likes kids," Amaris said when she and Grace were alone. "He went to the school with me today to hear my safety talk."

"He's so handsome! I'd be afraid to talk to him."

"Blake is so easy to talk to! Why, we can't seem to stop talking. Grace, I never knew any man who was so interesting."

"I'll bet he gets all the women's votes."

"He would make a wonderful governor," Amaris admitted. "That's the problem."

Grace gave her a questioning look.

"I would really like to develop a long-term relationship with him, but I'm not sure I could handle the lifestyle that goes along with him being governor."

"Are you saying he has proposed to you?" Grace's voice squeaked in her disbelief. "You hardly know each other."

"No. That's not what I mean. We do like each other a lot. And who knows where friendship might lead?"

"Amaris, you're usually levelheaded, but sometimes you don't look before you leap. I know I encouraged you to jump into this without thinking about it, but I think I was wrong to suggest that. Marriage can be really hard sometimes."

"I know. And I'm not rushing into anything. But I have thought about where this attraction we have for each other might lead, and frankly I'm worried about fitting into his world. Grace, he has a *butler*. And you should see his house. It's even more beautiful than the ones you see in the magazines. He raises horses that look to me like they're thoroughbreds. There's a Jacuzzi in his bathroom, and the tub and shower are in different stalls."

"How do you know what his bathroom looks like?"

Amaris ignored her. "You should have seen the people at his party. True, the party was a special one to solicit support from his primary opponents and unify the party for the upcoming election, but I have a feeling those people always dress in diamonds and emeralds, regardless of the occasion."

"Diamonds? Emeralds?"

"He has two houses. Eventide and a cabin on Long Hair Mountain. I don't even know anybody else with more than one car. He has three. He summers in Greece! His parents live in Switzerland!"

Grace looked as if she were reconsidering her recommendation for prudence. "You could learn to cope with all these things. I know I could! Think what it would be like to live like that!"

"But I don't know if I can! His world is nothing at all like mine."

"You can adjust, honey." Grace nodded firmly, as if she had made up her mind. "Don't let this one get away. Propose to him. Snap him up before he changes his mind."

"Grace! What about me not rushing into anything?"

"So rush. I gave you bad advice." Grace leaned nearer. "I know you're doing all right now, but once you get married things are more expensive. You need twice as many clothes, twice as much groceries, the movie costs double. When kids come along, the expenses soar. They eat constantly and outgrow clothes before they look even worn. You've seen how I have to scrimp and scrape to make ends meet. If you marry a rich man, you won't have these problems."

"I can't believe you're saying this."

"It's as easy to love a rich man as a poor one."

Amaris frowned. "If I did love him, it wouldn't be because of his money—it would be in spite of it."

"Take it from someone who's been there. Not having to worry about money, on top of everything else, will make a marriage easier."

"I think other things are more important."

"Like what?"

"My idea of riches is to have someone to love and be loved by in return. To have someone to share my life with, who will grow old beside me."

"Trust me. Fight growing old and go for money. You can hire a companion."

"I don't believe you mean a word of this." Amaris stood up and went to look out the window at the backyard. "Look at them. Blake should have sons of his own to play with."

Grace joined her. "He throws a football a whole lot straighter than Lyle. Maybe he really was on his college team."

"Blake wouldn't have said so if it wasn't true. He's like that. You can believe what he says."

"I didn't mean to imply he had lied about that. It's just that I find it hard to trust anything a man says these days."

"You're becoming a pessimist," Amaris chided with a friendly smile. "You should work on that." More seriously she added, "You know that will hamper the development of your psychic abilities."

Grace shrugged. "I don't have much time for that anymore. By the time I get home from work I'm too tired, and I have supper to cook and the house to clean. Besides, I'm not sure it's good for the boys to know I'm interested in that."

Amaris looked at her in surprise. "Why not?"

Grace didn't meet her eyes. "It confuses them. One of Ben's teachers called me and said Ben was trying to teach some of the other kids how to send thought pictures."

"Good for him."

"That's not the school's opinion. The principal thinks that sort of thing is satanic."

"What?" Amaris laughed. "That's ridiculous. Did you tell him he's wrong?"

"I told him Ben would stop talking about it. Don't look at me like that. The principal really scared me. He acted as if he thought I was an unfit mother or something. I can't afford for anyone to think that. Lyle would use that against me. He'd say it was more proof that I'm crazy and shouldn't have custody of the kids."

"Being psychic is simply another talent, like being able to sing or paint. Those of us who know that have an obligation to educate those who don't."

"You haven't had to face the school principal and argue the issue. It was easier to give in. And the only way I can be sure Ben quits talking about it at school is to stop him from doing it at home."

Amaris stared at her in disbelief. "Grace, what's gotten into you?"

"Maybe Lyle could have them taken away from me because of it. You know he says it's crazy to believe in it. He could cause trouble."

Amaris shook her head. "I don't know what to say. I never expected you to change how you feel about this. Ben and Todd have so much talent."

"They can develop an interest in sports or something else, like all the other boys. I don't want people thinking they're weird or that I raised them to be different."

"I think I should go. Blake and I have plans." Amaris knew she sounded cool, but she was hurt at what she felt Grace thinking. Grace was wishing that Amaris would stop challenging her decision to avoid the subject of her psychic gifts. Amaris didn't agree with Grace and never would. Grace's decision was wrong, and she knew Grace was aware of this.

At the door Amaris paused. "We aren't as close as we used to be. I miss that."

Grace nodded as if she were hesitant to admit it. "I know. People tell me divorce can cause that."

"Our friendship wasn't dependent on your being married."

"I've changed," Grace said almost defensively. "I've had to. It's not easy having to earn a living and raise two kids all alone."

Amaris was silent for a moment. "I miss the way we were."

After a pause Grace said, "I miss it, too, but I can't change the way things are. My life is different and so am I."

Amaris knew there was nothing to be said that would make matters different, because Grace was right. "We all change," she said at last. "I guess I have, too." She went out the back door to say goodbye to the boys.

Blake promised to come back and play ball with them again, and Amaris hugged them both, though Todd protested he was getting too old for that sort of thing. When she waved goodbye to Grace, her friend listlessly responded from behind the screen door.

They drove in relative silence to Amaris's house, and Blake sat on her bed while she packed her makeup and a change of clothes. "You're being awfully quiet all of a sudden. Are you having second thoughts?"

"No, it's Grace. I'm concerned about the changes see in her. She's become so skeptical and reserved. Sh says it's the divorce. Do you think that's true?"

"I don't know Grace, but I've seen my friend change as the result of something major like this hap pening in their lives."

"We had been working together on helping her boys develop their psychic abilities. Now she's discouraging it."

"She's their mother. She has a right to do that. Maybe they were getting carried away with it."

"She said Ben was giving lessons to the kids at school," Amaris said with a hint of a smile that quickly faded.

"There. You see?"

"I don't think anything is wrong with that."

"The parents of the other children might."

"Grace said the principal and Ben's teacher were less than pleased. They called it satanic. Can you believe there are still people who believe psychics are witches?"

"Apparently few people understand what it means to be psychic and most people fear the unknown."

Amaris pensively sat beside him on the bed. "Life can sometimes be hard to understand. I like Grace and want to continue being close friends with her, but her divorce has changed the way she looks at things. Now there are several issues getting in the way of our friendship, one of which is that she gets upset with me because I don't hate Lyle as she does. Each of them says the reason their marriage fell apart was because the other stopped loving them and then their own feelings died. Then Tiffany McNee came along and Lyle thought he loved her and that she loved him, and now they are no longer together and she's making goo-goo eyes at you."

"Hold it a minute. You're getting so wound up your spring may break. What does this woman making eyes at me have to do with your friends' marriage breaking up? Or is it that you are concerned that she'll come between us?"

Amaris thought for a moment before answering. What was really bothering her was Blake's earlier comment that implied he wasn't sure what it meant to be in love. "What I'm really curious about is…love."

Blake looked confused. "What do you mean? Everyone knows what love is."

"Earlier when I said I thought Tiffany didn't even know what love was, you said, 'Who does?'"

Blake averted his eyes. "I did? What a strange thing for me to say." Amaris could see that this discussion was making Blake feel uneasy. Was he still in love with Darla and couldn't admit it to himself? Suddenly Amaris wasn't sure whether that question had come from her mind or his, and instantly she raised her mental shield to block the influx of his thoughts. She had no business knowing his private thoughts or concerns.

Rising, Amaris cheerfully said, "Well, I guess I'm ready to go."

He stood and lifted her bag from the bed. "Do you have everything you need here?" He tried to appear as though nothing was bothering him, but Amaris heard the strain in his voice.

"You said to travel light. I'm assuming I won't be entertaining royalty or dressing for tea."

He gave her a suggestive look. "If all goes well you won't be dressing at all."

BLAKE'S MOUNTAIN CABIN had been built on a high grassy meadow overlooking one of the valleys. Partially surrounding the meadow and edging the south side of the house were tall hemlocks which were almost black against the clear sky. A hush lay over the meadow, but a breeze whispered in the trees. On close inspection, Amaris noticed the meadow was alive with the small creatures of the mountains. The breeze stirred her hair, and the rabbit she'd been watching warily hopped into hiding beneath the bending grasses.

"What serenity!" Amaris exclaimed. "I feel as if there could be no problems or worries here."

"I always feel the same way. Whenever I need to get away, I come here. Not many people know where it is, and I'm sure I'll be left alone." He looked thoughtfully at the aging cabin. "I suppose that will all change when I'm elected."

"Why?"

"There isn't even a phone here. If I'm governor I won't be able to be that secluded from my responsibilities. I suppose I could have a phone put in, but not having one is one of the charms of the place."

Amaris lifted her bag out of the trunk and waited for Blake to get his. "I never expected the cabin to be an old one. I thought it would look like Eventide, only made of logs."

"With a copy of Spenser in buckskins? I hope you aren't disappointed."

"No way. I love it here."

He led the way up the steps and across the porch. As he unlocked the heavy door, he said, "This place has a special past. It belonged to one of my great-grandfathers."

"I thought he married a Creole beauty and built Eventide."

"This one was on my mother's side of the family. Dad teases her about coming from peasant stock because, as nearly as we can tell, his family has always been wealthy." He went through the door on the far side of the room and put their suitcases in the bedroom. "It was originally built with only one room. The others were added as the family prospered."

"Somehow I suspected they had."

Blake shrugged as if it were only to be expected. "We've always been lucky, I guess. So far we've never had such a scoundrel or a wastrel in the family to decimate the fortune. We tend to invest in solid ventures."

"No gamblers?"

"None that were unlucky," he corrected. "That's how this branch of the family became wealthy. The son and heir was lucky at cards and knew when to leave the gambling table. He won controlling interest in a gold mine in Colorado and the land it sat on. Eventually the gold played out, but by then the land was beneath a town, and in time it became a major city. That proved more profitable than the mine."

Amaris looked around the comfortable but not richly appointed room. One wall was dominated by a large stone fireplace. A kitchen was in the opposite end of the room. In between was furniture which had apparently been chosen more for comfort than for style. It was clear that no interior decorator had ever set foot in the cabin.

Blake was stacking firewood on the blackened andirons in the fireplace. "The room feels damp and chilly now, but this will soon take care of that."

"You never cease to amaze me," she said as he ignited the kindling. "You even know how to build fire."

"Spencer isn't my constant nursemaid. I was also Boy Scout, you know."

"No, I didn't. That troop must have had some fine field trips: the Riviera, Bermuda, Paris."

"Now, now," he chided.

"Okay. But seriously, I wish I had known you when you were a boy. What were you like?"

"Like any other kid, I guess. I got in and out of scrapes all the time. What were you like?"

"I was a tomboy."

"I'd say you grew out of that rather well."

"Not entirely. I still prefer jeans to dresses. And you may have noticed that I still like to play Indians."

"Especially when you think someone will be shocked by it."

"Do I do that?" she asked in genuine surprise.

"Yes, you do. But you do it in a most delightful manner."

She was thoughtful as she watched the crackling fire leap around the lots. "I guess I do, at that. It's just that I think if someone is going to be offended by something I might say or do, it's better for me to know it up front, rather than worry about it."

He gave her an enigmatic smile.

"Well, it's true." She sighed. "Okay, so I like to shock people at times. I don't do it to be mean or to embarrass them."

"I know. That's what makes you delightful."

Amaris went to the window and peered out. After a while she said, "Did Darla like this cabin?" Amaris wasn't normally a jealous woman, but she felt a twinge at the thought of Blake sharing the big bed at Eventide with a woman other than herself—especially one he might still be subconsciously in love with.

"She was only here once. No, she didn't like it. Her entire visit lasted half an hour."

Amaris smiled out at the view beyond the window and hoped Blake didn't see her relief. At times psychometry was a definite drawback. "Good," she said.

Chapter Ten

Blake awoke early and rolled over to watch Amaris as she slept. She looked so vulnerable, yet he knew she possessed an inner strength that he admired and even envied at times. Her beautiful hair lay scattered around her head, its blue-black coloring in sharp contrast with the white pillowcase, and her eyelashes made a black fringe against her skin.

As Blake studied her, his thoughts turned to the discussion they had had prior to leaving her place the evening before. Amaris had brought up the subject of love. Her questions had been within the context of trying to understand the failed marriage of her friends, but she had repeated to him his unintentional quip that implied he wasn't sure anyone knew what love really was. Until Darla had broken his engagement, he had never questioned his understanding of love. But the past few weeks had changed all that. He could scarcely believe he had ever said such a thing, because now he knew exactly the meaning of love—it was Amaris. When he touched her or looked at her or listened to her voice, he felt a surge of love so powerful it shook him to the core of his being. He couldn't imagine a future without her in it.

He had thought he had been in love with Darla, he had agreed to marry her and had been faithful to her the entire time they had dated, and he had been prepared to remain faithful to her throughout their married life. But when she announced that she no longer loved him and in fact was already in love with another man, something inside Blake clicked, and it was as though his feelings of love for Darla had never existed. He felt no grief at the loss, no anger at being betrayed. He felt nothing. He had worried at the time that he might be incapable of love, but he knew now that he had not truly loved her in the first place. It was nothing at all like the love he felt for Amaris.

Gently he touched her face and traced her hairline past her temple and over her ear, then stroked his fingertips over the soft plane of her cheek. He and Amaris were friends as well as lovers. In fact their lovemaking was superb. But he also thoroughly enjoyed every moment they spent together. Amaris was intelligent and witty and often challenged his somewhat more traditional thinking with thought-provoking statements of her personal philosophy.

He had never known anyone with psychic abilities, if that label was appropriate to describe her particularly keen and accurate sense of intuition that had brought them together, and he was fascinated. Since the first day they had met, he had not given any thought to dating anyone but her. He had instinctively made that commitment to her, and he didn't feel the least bit confined by it as he had felt at times in his relationship with Darla. But what if Amaris didn't return his love? She was so enigmatic at times, so elusive, he couldn't be sure if she loved him or not. His love brought his vulnerability to the fore and he found himself afraid to speak of his love or to ask her how she felt toward him. Blake stroked her cheek again, and when he reached her lips she kissed his finger and opened her eyes.

For a long moment neither spoke as they lay gazing at each other with the smiles of lovers upon their lips, then Blake tilted his head and said, "Have I told you lately how beautiful you are? You are, you know." His deeply resonant voice was soft and gentle.

"What a wonderful way to start the day," she sighed. "And a more handsome man than you has never been born."

She closed her eyes and stretched, but when she opened her eyes she could see a troubled look behind Blake's smile. "Blake? Is something wrong?"

Blake's eyes darted back to hers. "Why do you ask?" The strain in his voice belied his lighthearted tone.

"If you think I'm eavesdropping on your thoughts, there is no need to worry. I told you before I wouldn't pry, even if I could be so selective. Is that what is bothering you?"

"Not any more. I trust you. But I think something has been bothering you lately."

"Maybe a little. I've been thinking more about our dating and how it might affect—"

Blake started shaking his head and interrupted her. "I don't want to hear any more about how my constituents or anyone else will be concerned that I'm dating someone I shouldn't. Unless, of course, you've got a criminal record you've been hiding from me." He grinned broadly to be sure she knew he was jesting.

Amaris returned his smile. "That wasn't what I was going to say. Let me try to explain. It's my psychic abilities I'm worried about. I consider them a God-given blessing, but there are many others who call it a curse. As a result, I have kept it all very quiet. Those people close to me, whom I can trust, know about me. But, for instance, the owner of the café where I work would likely fire me if he knew I was serious about psychic things—and he's my cousin.''

''Are you afraid I will tell someone and cost you your job?''

''No. That's not it at all. I'm worried that one of these nosy reporters who are always snooping around you will learn my secret and will ridicule you for your friendship with a weirdo and accuse you of being dependent on advice from 'Mother Amaris' or some such nonsense for your decision-making. I mean look at what happened when the media learned that President Reagan consulted an astrologer.''

''As I recall, it didn't hurt him much. There were quite a few jokes but I thought he weathered it all quite well.''

''But remember? He was already in his second term of office and wasn't eligible to run for reelection anyway.''

''Amaris. I think you are making much too much of this.''

''It's only because I care so much about you and your future.'' To keep him from seeing the worry in her eyes, she rolled away and wrapped herself in the voluminous white sheet as she left the bed. Out the window she could see the mists rising from the lower valley.

Blake came to stand behind her and put his arms around her. ''I didn't mean to chase you away.''

''I'm not running from you. I'm thinking.''

In silence he held her against his warmth as they watched the sun rise, dispelling the fog. "I suppose this is the way it must have looked even eons ago," he mused. "The mountains are always changing, yet they remain the same. You remind me of these mountains. You're so complex, yet you seem so straightforward."

"Am I complex? I suppose I am. I don't mean to be confusing."

"I know you don't mean to be, but I can't read your thoughts and I'm having a hard time figuring you out. I don't know why we can't just not talk about psychic things in public, and if some reporter gets wind of it from your past or from your other friends, you could simply tell them that you are open-minded and are studying such phenomena for the educational interest."

"You make it all sound so easy."

"Why shouldn't it be? I'm not a person to act on impulse, even if you couldn't prove it by my actions since I met you. I've given this a lot of thought, and the answer is clear to me. I care a great deal about you and I intend to spend just as much time as I can with you. If some of the voters don't understand, then so be it. I can't possibly please them all."

"You might not be elected."

"It's true that I'm up against stiff competition, but f I don't win it will likely be because of campaign is- sues, not personal ones."

Amaris turned and put her arms around his bare vaist. "I still say it's risky."

"Is that a psychic prediction?"

"What do you think?"

"I think it's foolish for two people who are of above verage intelligence to be standing here shivering when they could be cuddled together under the covers of that bed over there."

Amaris tried to look past the humor twinkling in his eyes. This was all happening fast and she wasn't sure Blake was being objective, but she cared so much for him she couldn't pull herself away from him—even for his own good.

"Come back to bed," he said softly. "I know your feet must be cold. Let me warm you up."

She let him lead her back to bed and snuggled next to his lean body. "You got pretty cold, too."

"I suppose I did. This old cabin doesn't have many of the amenities of home. No central heating or wall-to-wall carpeting. I hope it's not too uncomfortable for you here."

"I love this old cabin, because it's yours and you invited me to be here with you. I feel as if we were meant to be together, here, at this particular moment."

"And what about the moment following this?"

"I'm not good at predicting future events."

"It's just as well. If you could, there would be no surprises."

"Sometimes I think it would be better to know. Some surprises can be painful."

Blake pulled back, his expression serious. "You don't have a painful surprise for me, do you?"

"No, silly." She kissed his nose and then his lips. Amaris was touched by the vulnerability of this powerful man. She cared for him far too much to ever cause him pain. Hoping to shift his thoughts to another subject, she moved so that her bare breast grazed the back of his hand.

Blake took the gentle hint and began stroking the velvety skin of her breast and its pouting nipple. Sh excited him with her slender curves and eagerness to make love. They were as sexually compatible as if they had been lovers for years. "There is something you should know," he said.

At once her eyes became wide and vulnerable. "What is it?"

"I love you, Amaris. Something happened to me the first time I saw you. I know you're probably going to say it's too soon to know or..."

"No, I'm going to say I love you, too."

Blake could almost hear their hearts beating. "You do? Are you sure?"

"It's as if I always have, even before I knew you. I feel as if I've waited for you all my life."

Blake had never known such relief, nor such a profound happiness. He had thought he already loved her as much as he could, but his love was expanding until it filled him with its bright tenderness from head to toe. She loved him. His miracle had happened.

When he took her nipple into his mouth and bathed it with his tongue it immediately beaded tighter, and Amaris moaned softly in response. Knowing that he was pleasing her brought him even more satisfaction. He eased his hand lower over her supple skin until he found the treasure he sought. She parted her legs at the urging of his caress and he stroked her with his strong fingers until fires blazed in the center of her being.

Amaris murmured his name, returning his loving caresses in kind, and soon Blake's desire raged as if they had not spent most of the night before making love. He wanted her with a primitive urgency that became a need as her hands and lips pledged him promises that he was certain she was eager to keep.

When he became one with her, he had to fight to restrain himself.

Beneath him was the most desirable woman in his world, and she loved him as he loved her. Her hair was spread across the pillow in an ebony cascade. Her eyes were dark silver with passion, her lips rosy and swollen from his kisses. As he began to move within her, her breasts swayed in the rhythm of his loving. He lowered his torso so that her nipples trailed fire across his chest.

As he brought her nearer to her peak, he gathered her closer and let their hot skin kiss from head to toe. Amaris caught her breath as he took one nipple between his thumb and forefinger and rolled it gently.

All at once he felt her grow tighter around him and her breath quickened. Excitement plunged through him as he realized how close she was to her pinnacle, yet he prolonged the ecstasy until she cried out for release. Then, letting himself enjoy her fully, he moved with her toward the culmination of their loving. When he felt her rhythmic waves of completion, his fulfillment was triggered, and together they rode on the crest of love.

For long moments they floated in golden bliss, too out of breath and too full of love and satisfaction to speak. Blake felt so close to her he was sure his hear was beating in unison with hers and their thoughts were entwined. Never had he felt such unity with another person.

In the peace and serenity of their afterglow, they le the world spin by without them for the few minute they had left before the alarm he'd set would go of sending him back onto the campaign trail again.

ALTHOUGH BLAKE CALLED Amaris each evening he was away, his plans had changed on the road, and instead of him being gone two days, it had extended to five. Amaris found herself unable to write her short stories or to do anything except think about Blake. It was no longer enough to pass her time enjoying the vivid autumn colors of the mountain or to fashion a vest using an authentic Indian weave. She wanted nothing more than to be with Blake, but when her dreams embroidered him into her future, the fantasy of love and marriage was clouded by her concern that she would never be able to adjust to the fishbowl life-style of a politician and her fear that his chances to become governor might be ruined because of his association with a woman who could read more from a newspaper than the printed words.

On his return, she'd met his plane at Woodrum Field in Roanoke, and he'd taken her to his cabin. But the next day he had to leave again, and although he'd offered to take her with him, she knew their time together would be severely limited and had declined. But every moment her thoughts were on him.

"He's becoming an obsession," Amaris told Grace over hot chocolate and brownies in Grace's kitchen. "Even when he's gone as much as he has been here lately, I can't think of anything but him. I don't even want to think of anything else."

"If I were you, I wouldn't want to either."

Amaris took a bite out of a brownie and methodically chewed and swallowed it before she said, "I'm in love with him."

Grace leaned forward eagerly. "Hey, that's great! Has he asked you to marry him?"

"Not yet, but I have a feeling he will, and then what am I going to do? I'm so confused."

"Are you crazy? Men like Blake Mayfield don't come along every day! Tell him you'll marry him and work out your doubts later."

"Grace! How can you suggest such a thing. I have to be positive it will work out before I can say yes. He's already been hurt by one woman who told him she loved him, accepted his marriage proposal, then dumped him for someone else."

"I know the feeling," Grace commiserated. "But if you don't say you'll marry him, he may lose interest in you. Besides, you say you love him."

"I do. I love him more than I ever thought it was possible to love anyone. But what if we marry and I discover I detest such a public life? You know how I've always needed my privacy and how I've always said I'm not happy living away from the mountains. I may not be any good as a governor's wife. They have to do their share of politicking, too, you know. I don't think I can do that." She paused and added, "But I also don't think I can do without him."

"Would you listen to yourself? Amaris, the only way to be happy is to make yourself happy, and take it from one who's been there—it's a lot easier with money than it is without it. The same goes for companionship. Lord knows Lyle wasn't much, but he was better than an empty house. Blake is handsome and sexy and best of all, he's rich. If I were you, I'd snap him up before he had time to turn around."

"I don't believe that. Not if you really had to make the choice."

"How hard can it be to learn to be a governor's wife? You go to luncheons, a few grand openings—you can learn all that easy enough."

Amaris rested her chin in her palm. "The point is that I'm not sure I would be comfortable living in his world. You know how bad I am about saying what I really think. My opinions just pop out of my mouth. Can you imagine how well that would go over in a politician's wife?"

"You did all right in that interview with Laura Irving. According to her article, you could easily have been a consort of Abraham Lincoln."

"That's only one reporter, and she was kind. Someone else could have taken that same information and ripped me to shreds. It was risky of me to talk to her at all, but I was so upset with Blake's campaign manager, I wasn't thinking clearly."

"A smart campaign manager could make you seem so down-home American that the voters would feel guilty about not voting for Blake."

"Maybe one who liked me could, but Jeff sees me as a threat. I think he's truly disliked me from the minute we met. I've tried to overlook his innuendos that I'm trying to ruin Blake's career, but it isn't easy."

"Does Blake know what Jeff is doing?"

"He's got a pretty good idea, but I don't want to cause trouble between him and Blake. Not only is Jeff Blake's campaign manager and right-hand man, he's Blake's best friend."

"If they're such good friends, maybe Jeff is jealous of you."

Amaris tilted her head to one side. "I never thought of that. But he says he is only looking out for Blake's political interests." Amaris sighed. "Besides, Jeff may

be right. I may not be good for his career. I don't think
I could be a politician's wife. Not a good one, anyway.
And if it ever gets out that he'd married a psychic, he'd
be in duck soup.''

''Don't talk like that,'' Grace scolded. ''No one will
ever know you're psychic. Besides, any woman in her
right mind would kill to be in your position. Not only
is Blake handsome, he's a *millionaire.*''

''More important than that, I love him and he loves
me.''

Grace shook her head. ''I don't understand you. It
seems to me you're making all this much harder than
it needs to be. You love him. He loves you. That
sounds simple to me. Next thing you know, he'll propose and you can marry him. You can work out the
details later.''

''His career isn't an insignificant detail. If he becomes the governor, we'll have to live in Richmond,
and if he someday is elected to a national office, we'll
have to move to Washington. I love these mountains
and I don't want to move.''

Grace went to the sink to wash out her cup, shaking
her head in dismay. ''It sounds to me like you're
scared. If it were me, I'd marry him before he got the
proposal out of his mouth, love or no love.''

''Try telling that to someone who doesn't know you
as well as I do.''

''You haven't had to struggle to make ends meet the
way I've had to.''

Amaris also got to her feet and carried her cup to the
sink. ''Blake just got back home about an hour ago.
He says he's going to be here for three days this time
and he asked if he could come see me after he finished
his meetings this afternoon. But instead I offered to g

see him so he wouldn't have to drive. He's been on the road so much lately.''

"While you're there, I want you to say, 'Blake Mayfield, I love you. Let's get married.' ''

"I told you before, I'm not going to rush into anything."

Amaris picked up her purse and headed out through the living room where Ben and Todd were watching cartoons. "I think I'll stop by Jeff's office and try to work something out with him." To the boys she said, "I'm leaving, now. Can I have a hug?"

Todd gave her an abbreviated squeeze, his eyes still glued to the TV set, but Ben launched himself at her and exuberantly hugged her. As Amaris returned his embrace, she felt a twinge of apprehension.

Her eyebrows knitted in mild concern and she asked, "Ben, do you feel okay?"

"Yep. I feel keen-o."

"Hurray for cartoons," his mother said wryly.

Amaris released the boy, shaking off her uneasiness. He looked perfectly well, as did Todd. She straightened and put the feeling aside. There was nothing wrong at all. No doubt this uneasy feeling was related to her worry over what to do about Blake.

On her way to Jeff Hancock's office a light rain began falling, and thunder rumbled harmlessly in the distance. Another cold front was passing through, and soon the snows would come. When she parked out front she was relieved to note only two cars were there: Jeff's white Lincoln and one which probably belonged to his secretary. Getting her courage up to speak to Jeff in private hadn't been easy, and on the way it occurred to her that as busy as the campaign was these days, Jeff might not be alone.

Just as she stepped through the doorway of the office building, the rain began to fall in earnest. A woman who appeared to be in her mid-fifties looked up from her paperwork as Amaris entered and peered over the top of her glasses. "May I help you?" she asked with professional politeness.

"May I see Jeff Hancock?"

"Do you have an appointment?"

"No, I don't. My name is Amaris Channing."

The secretary pursed her lips as if she would rather send Amaris on her way, but instead pressed the button on her intercom and spoke into the phone. "There's a Ms. Channing to see you, Mr. Hancock."

After a pause, she hung up the receiver and said, "You may go back. Mr. Hancock's office is directly behind me."

Amaris nodded her thanks and stepped around the reception desk to the hall the woman had indicated. Among numerous vacant offices, one was clearly marked "J. D. Hancock." Amaris opened the door and let herself in.

Jeff sat behind a massive walnut desk, one corner of which was topped with neat stacks of brochures and folded pamphlets. On the wall behind him were three mock-ups of posters promoting Blake Mayfield for governor. Three small television sets were mounted in the opposite wall. He looked busy, and not at all pleased to see her.

"I'm sorry to disturb you," Amaris said. "I suppose I should have called first."

"That would have been more convenient. You might have missed me. I have a meeting across town in an hour."

Amaris was surprised by his brusqueness, but couldn't tell whether he was angry with her or merely upset at the unexpected intrusion. "What I have to say won't take long."

"Sit down," he said belatedly. "What can I do for you?"

"I've come to try to make peace between us for Blake's sake."

"Make peace? I don't understand," Jeff said with determined obtuseness.

"Yes, you do. You've made it clear you don't like me, and I'm trying not to feel the same way about you. I'm afraid that animosity is going to hurt Blake if he finds out. And he surely will."

Jeff tapped the eraser of his pencil on the desktop. "And what makes you so certain? Have you told him of our conversations?"

"He knows we've spoken, but I haven't told him what about. That was between the two of us. But Blake and I have every intention of continuing our friendship and I know you are adamantly opposed to him having a relationship with me. So unless you intend to quit your job and stop being his friend, which by the way I hope you don't, we have a problem to work out."

Jeff leaned back in his leather chair, speculatively regarding her. "Are you aware he has only recently broken off his engagement with Darla Radborne?"

"Yes, but that has nothing to do with you and me." After a brief pause, she asked, "Are you suggesting there is still something between them?"

"I didn't say that. I only wanted to be sure you were aware of the facts."

"Blake told me that she broke the engagement with him."

"My point is that Darla was perfectly matched to Blake, both socially and politically."

"And I'm not? Is that what you mean? In my opinion you aren't his best choice as campaign manager, but since I'm trying to call a truce I'll refrain from pointing that out."

"I believe you just did."

"Perhaps I was foolish to think you and I could ever be friends, but we really must learn to tolerate one another."

"Look," Jeff said, leaning his forearms on his desk. "Personally I have nothing against you. I only feel you are the wrong person for Blake to date at this time. We're getting ready to spearhead a campaign for Blake's election against an incumbent governor, and it's going to be rough. Now, you don't have to be a political genius to see that Blake needs to have everything in his favor and to have all his attention focused on business right now."

"I can understand that."

"I thought so. Now—"

"But it doesn't change how matters stand. Unless Blake changes his mind, we will continue dating, and unless you change your opinion of me and my suitability for Blake, you and I will remain at odds."

Jeff leaned back in his chair and drew a deep breath. "Miss Channing, you're right. We shouldn't fight. Much too much is at stake here. I've known Blake since we were kids. His family has a lengthy heritage of public service and pride. The time has come for Blake to enter politics and carry forward a tradition that began generations ago. Blake is an intensely proud man who hates to admit he's made a mistake. If you care fo him as you say you do, take my advice and step out of his life—at least for now.''

''I didn't come here for advice,'' she said as she rose to go. ''I came here hoping you and I could reach an understanding, but I see that's impossible.''

Jeff expression was suddenly dark with rage and obvious frustration. For a moment he rubbed his furrowed brow, and then he looked directly into her eyes and asked, ''You want money? Is that it?''

She was too astounded to answer.

He reached into the lap drawer of his desk and took out a checkbook. ''How much?'' he demanded.

Amaris's eyes flashed silver fire as she drew herself up. ''I don't want money. I can't believe you would even suggest such a thing.''

''Believe it,'' Jeff said in exasperation. ''Will five thousand be enough? Ten?''

For a minute Amaris considered throwing something at him, but she had never been one to lose her temper easily. ''I'm going to pretend you never tried to bribe me to stay away from Blake. Otherwise we will never resolve this. You think about what I said, and see if you have enough friendship for Blake to give a bit. Next time you can come to me.'' With a toss of her head, Amaris turned and left the room. She took pleasure in slamming the door so hard the windows rattled down the hall.

As she entered the lobby, the receptionist stared at her as if she wasn't sure whether to hide under her desk or run for help. Amaris forced a smile to her lips as she left the building, hoping to ease the woman's concern.

Through the continuing downpour, Amaris dashed across the parking lot to the haven of her car. Now she was drenched, on top of being angry. This wasn't going to be her day, unless something changed soon. Through the raindrops that clung to her eyelashes, she looked back into the lighted interior of Jeff Hancock's office building. The receptionist had returned to her typing as though nothing had happened, and Amaris wished she could ignore the unpleasantness as easily but she knew she was too entangled to do so.

As she turned her car out onto the street a bit too fast, the rear tires broke traction, startling her. As quickly as she'd lost control, she regained it, and at the same time she realized that her anger at Jeff had been threatening to overcome her better judgment. She had considered telling Blake that Jeff had tried to pay her off but now knew she shouldn't. Blake would take a dim view of Jeff's actions and she didn't want to come between Blake and his best friend. Besides, Jeff's arguments made sense. A politician's life was no longer his own and there was more at stake than their personal happiness.

As she was waved through Blake's security gates by his guard, she wasn't surprised that the panoramic view of the mountains and valley beyond the mansion were obscured by the pewter sheets of rain. Even the house itself was barely visible through the downpour.

Spenser met her at the door and showed her into the back parlor. The furniture, covered in a rose print on a background of deepest green, looked as comfortable as that in the rest of the house yet was not as formal. Above the fire that crackled cozily in the hearth, a mantel clock ticked softly.

Blake was sitting at his desk, intently studying a handful of typewritten sheets. When he saw Amaris, he put aside the papers and came to her. After a lingering kiss that threatened to curl her toes, he drew back and held her at arm's length. "I can't tell you how much I enjoy seeing you come into a room. It's as if you belong here. I love you."

"I love you, too, but I must look like a drowned rat. It's pouring out there. I hope I'm not interrupting something important."

"Not at all, and you look beautiful. I'm glad you're here. I was just revising one of my speeches. It can wait."

Blake motioned for her to be seated in an overstuffed chair facing the fire. Taking his place in the chair opposite her, he pulled off her wet shoes, then began vigorously massaging her cold feet. "You look beautiful but why aren't you wearing boots on a day like this?"

"It wasn't raining when I left my house." She relaxed into the comfortable chair and let the enjoyment of his foot rub relax her. "You have no idea how good that feels."

"I appreciate your coming over. But if I'd known it was going to rain, I'd have insisted you let me come to your place."

"I've been thinking about you all day."

"You're on my mind a lot, too. Jeff keeps me running pretty hard these days, but my thoughts constantly turn to you."

Blake tucked her feet into the warm spot between his thigh and the arm of the chair as Spenser brought each of them a cup of steaming cider. When they were alone again, Blake said, "I used to look forward to getting back home, but now Eventide is lonely without you."

"My house is empty without you in it."

"We could change all that," he said with a smile. "Amaris, I want you to be my wife. Will you marry me?"

Amaris had thought he would propose marriage to her someday, but she hadn't expected it to be so soon. She pulled her feet back and tucked them under herself. After gazing into the fire for a long moment, she spoke. "I talked to Grace today."

"Oh? What does that have to do with my question?"

"She told me that if you were to ask me to marry you, I should take you up on it before you get away."

"I like Grace."

Amaris smiled at his response, despite the concern she was feeling. "But what she meant was that I should marry your money."

Blake's smile faded and his expression became serious. "I didn't ask you to—"

"I know, Blake. But it's not just Grace. If we married, others would think that I married you for your money and that would bother me a great deal."

Blake's brows knitted. "Are you talking about someone in particular?"

Amaris had been thinking of Jeff, but knew it would hurt Blake if she told him what had happened less than an hour before. "Blake, it's all so very complicated."

Blake rose to his feet. "Honey, life doesn't have to be so difficult. You and I are single and in love. What could be simpler than for us to be married?"

"You aren't that naive, Blake. No one is."

He threw up his hands and went back to his chair. "What will it take for you to marry me? Should I give all I own to charity? Sell Eventide? Get a job doing manual labor? Just tell me."

She shook her head and sighed. ''I don't want you to do any of those things. Eventide, and all that it represents, is what has made you the way you are. I don't want to change that.''

She knelt beside his chair and put her hands on his knees. ''The problem is in me, not you. I love you too much to be selfish. I have to consider what marriage to me will do to your future.''

''It would make me damned happy,'' he growled.

''I don't mean just your personal future, but your political future as well.''

Blake met her eyes squarely. ''If you aren't by my side, I don't know if I could be content being president, governor or even dogcatcher.''

Amaris put her arms about his waist and held her body to his. Blake returned the embrace. Tears formed behind her lids and spilled down her cheeks, but Amaris didn't bother to brush them away. She saw no way out of her quandary and she thought it was quite reasonable for her to cry about it. Even if she could resolve her own feelings about living in the public eye—and she hoped that in time she could—that wouldn't change the issue of what the voters would think about her. She would become an embarrassment to Blake if her psychic abilities became known. Since she had never gone to any lengths to hide them up until now, she knew a clever reporter could easily discover her interests. In time, especially if she cost him the presidency, she believed Blake might come to resent her. By then it would be too late. Blake had his pride and his destiny to fulfill. What she was going to do about all this, she didn't know.

Chapter Eleven

Amaris was nervous as she and Blake went down th
curving stone steps to the patio. The house was owne
by one of the staunchest supporters of Blake's politi
cal party and this outdoor cookout was to garner mor
financial support for Blake's campaign. Many of th
people invited represented Virginia's oldest and mos
elite families and Amaris was surprised that she rec
ognized many of the faces from newspapers and mag
azines. She felt extremely intimidated amid thes
illustrious people and she could hardly walk down th
steps for fear of somehow doing something that migh
embarrass him. Blake, as usual, seemed perfectl
within his element. "Don't you ever get nervous?" sh
whispered as they neared the stone-paved patio.

"Of course." He grinned and waved at a familia
face. "The trick is never to show it."

She put on a smile and reminded herself to breath
as the people turned their attention to Blake and her
self. She saw Jeff and managed not to let his accusin
glare cause her any visible discomfort. Blake loved her
The miracle that he wanted her and returned her lov
was enough to strengthen her resolve. With him besid
her, she could do anything. She lifted her head an

stepped away from the last step, but her heel caught on a rough part of stone and she let out a startled cry as she fell forward.

Blake was there before she hit the ground, his strong arms about her. She leaned against him as she regained her balance, if not her composure.

"Are you all right?" he asked, his anxious eyes searching her face.

"Yes. Yes, of course I am." Her ankle ached and she felt as if she might die of embarrassment, but she wasn't about to admit it. "I've heard it's good to make a memorable entrance." She was relieved to hear chuckles from the people who were near enough to overhear her.

Blake gave her a look of such love, her embarrassment faded. With her hand tucked into his arm, she made her way through the introductions and polite conversation.

Although she tried to remember the names and faces of all those she was meeting, she found herself nodding and smiling and mouthing the proper responses, yet forgetting the names almost as fast as she heard them. Remembering names and connecting them with the correct faces had never been her strong suit, and she now regretted never having developed this ability. Everyone there seemed to know everyone else intimately, and they all knew her name because of her connection with Blake. As the introductions continued, she made a greater effort to memorize the names and faces.

When the reached the canapé table, Amaris eased behind the linen tablecloth and slipped her foot out of her shoe to flex her sore ankle. It felt as if it might be swelling and she thought she should get her weight off it, but there was nowhere in sight to sit down. Thus, she left off her shoe and rested her foot against the cool stones of the patio. At least, she noticed, Jeff was staying away. In her present state of discomfort, she wasn't sure she could handle a conversation with him.

As she watched Blake exchange pleasantries with the seemingly unending string of people who sought him out, she again felt an unpleasant surge of shyness. Amaris had always been a private sort of person who required large amounts of solitude and had only allowed a few of her closest friends to know her more intimate thoughts and feelings. All these people crowding around Blake seemed to know everything about him and he didn't appear to mind that at all. In fact, he seemed to know as much about them as they all did about him. Once again, Amaris found herself wondering if she could ever allow so many people access to her world and whether she would be happy without her privacy.

Blake had told her he loved her and had proposed. She loved him. That much was straightforward and simple. But if she married Blake, she would also marry his career, and that involved a serious decision.

She turned her head to look beyond the patio at the undulating mountains. As always, she derived a sense of peace and strength from them—as if the mountains were her talisman. If she married Blake and if he became governor, could she leave the serenity of her mountains and move to a city? Could she ever be happy at all in a place where cars and people outnumbered the trees?

She looked back at Blake. Could she ever be happy away from him? She knew the answer to that question was a definite no. Amaris never gave her love lightly when she loved, she loved totally. Blake was more important to her than anything. Yet to go with him into public life, she would have to give up a large portion of herself.

As if he sensed her discomfort, Blake put his arm around her waist and said softly, "You look tired. Come with me."

Amaris shoved her foot back into her shoe and tried to walk without limping as Blake escorted her toward a sloping walk that led down to an artificial pond. To her relief, she saw a stone bench at the water's edge.

"You looked as if you needed a breather," he said. "Sometimes crowds can do that to a person."

"I was beginning to feel a bit claustrophobic," she admitted. "But we can't stay here. You have to get back up there and mingle."

"We'll go back soon."

Amaris sank down on the bench and sighed with relief.

"Are you sure you didn't hurt yourself on the steps? You seemed to be having difficulty walking."

"It's nothing. Sitting down for a few minutes will take care of it." She looked at the lily pads floating on the pond's still surface. Here and there were orange and white flashes of Koi fish darting about in the dark water.

"Everyone is wondering who you are," Blake said as he took her hand in his. He ran his thumb over her skin as their fingers laced together.

"Well, why should I be the only one who wonders that?" she teased him with a smile. "I used to know who I was, but these last few days I'm not so sure. Falling in love with you had made me more complete somehow, but at the same time it has turned my world upside down. Does that make sense?''

''It does to me. I feel the same way. You put sunshine in my life.''

Amaris glanced over her shoulder at the group of richly dressed people. ''You weren't exactly living a cheerless existence before I came along.''

''No, but it seems that way in retrospect. I didn't realize how much I was missing until I met you. Until I fell in love with you.'' He cupped her cheek in the palm of his hand. ''I can't imagine a life without you.''

Amaris could feel his thoughts in her own mind and the depth of his love made her lips part in surprise. He loved her enough to give up everything for her. Everything. He loved her as much as she loved him. And with that knowledge came a grave responsibility. To allow him to give up his life in the public eye would be as impossible for her as it would be for her to stop loving him.

''Have you made up your mind about marrying me?'' Blake asked, his deep voice caressing her soul.

Her eyes searched his as she tried to think what to say. She wanted to marry him. She wanted to wake up every morning next to him and to read the Sunday paper together and to have the thousands of relatively unimportant memories that made up a marriage. But she and Blake were so different when it came to goals and life-styles. Could she be happy in his world? How could she ever have the privacy that was so essential to her if she was the wife of a governor?

''Amaris?'' he asked with concern darkening his eyes.

''Yes, yes, I heard you. I—''

"No. Don't answer now. You said you needed time to think. I shouldn't have asked you again so soon. It's just that I love you and I hadn't expected your answer to require so much thought."

"And I love you!" Amaris caught his hands between hers and her eyes begged him to understand. She couldn't tell him she was reluctant to marry his political aspirations as well. He might renounce his future for her, and in time he might regret it. Regret could be poison to love. "It's a big decision, Blake." She saw the confused hurt in his eyes and knew she couldn't do anything about it. She couldn't make a snap decision that would affect the rest of their lives. "Give me a little more time," she said softly.

Blake wished he could say that he understood, but he didn't. The one thing he was sure of, though, was that he didn't want to lose Amaris by pushing her too hard. "I'll give you all the time you need." She was often such a mixture of seeming contradictions. "I love you, Amaris. I won't press you into a quick decision."

Faintly she smiled, and he had to restrain himself from taking her into his arms right then and there.

To Blake she had become the center of his universe. There were countless places he wanted to take her, so much he wanted to show her. He knew and shared her love of the mountains, and if she but asked him to do it, he would drop out of the gubernatorial race and never look back. He had never thought he could love a woman, any woman, that much.

When Blake and Darla had broken up he had at first felt angry and hurt, but quickly he became amazed how little he felt toward her at all. Amaris's reluctance to agree to marry him plunged him into an abyss he had never felt with Darla. He knew now he hadn't been devastated over the loss of Darla simply because he had loved the idea of her and not her as a woman. He loved Amaris to the depths of his soul and vowed to himself that he would wait forever for her, if need be.

Together, they rose and walked back up the incline to the party.

TWO DAYS LATER, Amaris answered the knock on her front door to find no one there. On the doorknob, however, was a plastic bag and in the bag was one of the papers that could be found at all the supermarket checkout counters. She opened the paper to the front page and was astounded to find a photo of herself, mouth open, eyes wide and falling forward as Blake tried to catch her.

Her mouth dropped open in shock. Above the photograph were the words. "Mayfield's Secret Lover Sets Fund-raiser on Ear." Below that she was quoted as saying, "I always like to make a memorable entrance."

Her fingers were suddenly cold and she felt vaguely sick at her stomach as she thumbed through the tabloid for the story. On page four was another picture of her at the canapé table, standing with one shoe off. Across the table a couple were talking with Blake and by the expressions captured, a casual observer would clearly take it to mean that Amaris was the cause of their frowns. She recalled the couple well. They had sported unpleasant expressions all evening, even when one or the other was telling a joke.

A smaller photo showed Amaris gazing off at the mountains as if she were thoroughly bored with the party. The accompanying story was along the same lines the photos suggested.

With a groan, Amaris wadded up the paper and sank down onto her couch. She closed her eyes and tried not to think of all the copies of this tabloid in public view throughout the state. She felt as if her privacy had not only been invaded but raped. And who had hung the gossip rag on her doorknob, knocked and then run away? She had thought she didn't have an enemy in the world.

Wadding the paper into a ball, she threw it with all her pent-up anger into the fire that crackled on her hearth. As it caught flame and began to burn, she lay back on the couch. As a governor's wife, she would be subject to this sort of muckraking all the time. Indeed, after this article, she could be a distinct disadvantage to Blake's campaign.

Yet, how could she bear to leave him? But how could she stay?

GRACE SHIFTED HER BAG of groceries from one arm to the other as she fumbled in her purse for her key. She wasn't in a particularly good mood and her feet ached because she'd worn a new pair of shoes to work which weren't yet broken in. She had been a day late in getting to the grocery store and thus had missed the sale on ground beef. There had been a long line at the checkout counter and the girl working the cash register was a new trainee who had moved like cold molasses. Further, two of her items had no price on them, so she'd had to wait while an equally slow stock boy sauntered back to check the prices. By the time she had left the grocery store, she was fuming.

Then her car had given her trouble. The ignition switch was wearing out, and she'd had to jiggle the key half a dozen times before the car would start. And that meant another unexpected expense. The depression that had been lingering around her since cold weather had come was settling upon her by the time she reached home.

As she unlocked the door and elbowed it open, she wondered why her boys could never figure out she needed help when she had been to the grocery store. "I'm home," she called out. She could hear the television going in the living room, but neither boy answered her greeting.

Grace set the heavy bag onto the countertop. "Boys, I'm home." On her way back out for another load, she said, "Come help me carry in the groceries."

As she was coming back in with her arms full, she was peeved. Todd and Ben were getting old enough to help out more around the house, yet when they had their eyes glued to the television it was almost impossible for her to get their attention.

Still fuming, Grace carried all the groceries into the house, then after putting them away she went to the living room to scold her sons.

The television was on, its screen casting flickering lights into the dim room, but her sons weren't sprawled in front of it as she'd expected. Grace turned on the living-room light and verified that the room was indeed empty.

With a frown, she turned off the TV and loudly called out, "Todd? Ben? Where are you?"

There was no answer, and without the noise from the television the house was eerily quiet. "Todd?" she called with more concern. "Ben?"

When there was again no answer Grace headed up stairs, telling herself there was no reason to be wo ried. If the boys were upstairs playing, they wouldn't necessarily have heard her.

When she pushed open the door to their room, her heart froze. The closet door was open and all their clothes were gone, as were most of their toys, including Bugs and Bear—Ben's favorites. "Ben?" Her voice sounded small through her fear-constricted throat. "Todd?" she called out much more loudly. Her first thought was that Lyle had taken them, but denial quickly erased the notion from her mind; she could not face her worst fear. The boys had to be here at home, safely at home. "Are you boys playing games with me?"

She ran to her own bedroom, but it was empty as well. Panic had sent her thoughts skittering. Outside. They weren't supposed to be out after dark, but they must be playing outside!

Grace ran downstairs and out the front door. Evening had settled over the valley and lights were burning in all the windows of her neighbors' houses. A wet chill hung in the air and clouds hid the moon and the stars. "Todd!" she shouted. "Ben, come here!"

When only silence came back, Grace hurried to her nearest neighbor's house and knocked on the door. When the woman answered, Grace said, "Jean. Have you seen Todd and Ben?"

Jean shook her head. "No, we were just about to sit down to supper. They aren't over here." She called back into the house, "Jason, have you seen Todd and Ben?"

A child's voice answered, "Not since school was out."

Jean shook her head again. "Sorry. Have you tried the Kellermans?"

"No, but I will. Thanks." Grace forced a smile to her lips. She didn't want her nosy neighbor knowing she was scared half to death.

In short order she learned that the Kellermans hadn't seen them, and neither had the O'Maras or the Dobsons. None of the other neighbors had children.

Grace searched the house again, leaving her sons' bedroom for last. As she stood in their doorway, staring into the void in their closet where their clothing had been, her eyes filled with tears. The boys were gone and she felt sure Lyle had taken them. She picked up the phone to call him but couldn't follow through. She was terribly afraid Lyle had taken them out of anger and she'd never see them again. And even worse, she couldn't bear the thought that he hadn't, for that would mean someone else had kidnapped them. With trembling fingers, she dialed Amaris's number.

Amaris answered on the second ring. "Hi, Grace. You just caught me. Blake and I were on our way to Roanoke to see a play."

"I'm sorry to disturb you," Grace said as she fought hard to keep her voice steady. "Todd and Ben aren't here." The hot tears that stung Grace's eyes spilled onto her cheeks. "They're...well, they aren't here."

"Grace, are you trying to tell me they're missing?"

"Yes," she sobbed.

Amaris covered the mouthpiece of the phone and said to Blake, "Grace says the boys are missing."

"Missing? What does she mean missing?" His brows furrowed in concern.

"She sounds as if she's crying." Turning back to the phone, Amaris asked, "Grace, have you checked at Jason's house?"

"Of course. I've looked everywhere, but—"

"We'll be right over," Amaris interrupted.

"No, no," Grace said with a sniff. "You have plans, I'll—"

"Nonsense. We'll be there in a few minutes." Amaris hung up and said to Blake. "I hope you don't mind. Grace sounded really upset."

"Certainly not." He had already taken her wrap from the chair and was draping it around her shoulders.

As they approached Grace's neighborhood, Amaris concentrated her attention on the darkened sidewalks in hopes of catching a glimpse of the boys. All day she had worked on building her courage to talk with Blake about her concerns and the difficulty she was having in responding to his proposal, and she had rehearsed the words in her mind so often she felt relief with this diversion. She didn't think the boys were really missing—Grace always jumped to conclusions where they were concerned. She felt sure they would find the boys, then she would still have several hours to talk with Blake before the evening was over.

Grace was waiting for them on her porch. "Have they shown up yet?" Amaris asked, though from Grace's expression she could tell they hadn't.

Grace tightened her lips to keep from crying and shook her head.

At Blake's urging they all went into the living room and Grace tried to tell Amaris and Blake all that had happened, but she was barely coherent.

"The TV was on?" Blake asked, trying to better determine the facts.

Grace nodded. "They never remember to turn it off."

"Were the doors locked?"

"I don't know. I mean…I think so." Grace clenched her hands together in her lap. "I didn't really notice. I assumed they were. The boys know to stay inside and keep the doors locked after dark." Her voice broke and her face crumpled. "Why did I stop off at the grocery store today of all days? If I'd come straight home, Lyle wouldn't have been able to take them from me."

"Lyle? Are you sure?"

"Their clothes and a lot of their toys are gone, too, and it's all my fault."

Amaris put her arm around Grace to comfort her. "You aren't to blame for anything. Have you called Lyle?"

Grace vigorously shook her head from side to side. "I'm afraid to. If they aren't there…" Her voice trailed off.

Amaris went to the phone in the kitchen and dialed Lyle's number. After a dozen rings, she concluded no one was home.

Grace's haunted eyes followed her back into the room. "He's not home, is he?" Grace asked. Amaris shook her head.

"Maybe he took the boys to a movie," Blake suggested.

"He's not allowed to do that. Lyle knows he can only see the boys here," she forcefully jabbed her finger down at the rug, "and only when I'm home."

"I had no idea our courts had become so stringent," Blake commented.

"The court isn't. *I* am. If he won't pay child support, he can't see them whenever and however he chooses!"

Blake's eyes met Amaris's. "Maybe we ought to drive over to Lyle's house. He may be home but not answering the phone," she suggested.

Grace stood up to go with them, but Amaris gently detained her. "I think you should stay here in the event they come home. It's still possible they're outside playing and are just late coming in." Amaris could see that Grace was in no shape to confront Lyle face-to-face.

"With all their clothes and toys?" Grace sobbed. "Lyle has taken them! I know he has!"

"We don't know that for sure. Stay here, in case the boys call to say where they are." After Grace reluctantly nodded, Amaris and Blake left.

At Lyle's garage apartment, Amaris's heart sank. All the lights were out and Lyle's car was not in the driveway. She knew Blake had also noticed the place looked vacant. Nevertheless, he knocked loudly on the door. As they waited for an answer, Amaris turned all her senses to the apartment. No one was there. She was sure of it. No thoughts met her probing mind.

Through a window on a small porch, she peered in. "I can't see much, but it looks as if he may have moved."

"That's not good news."

They went to the house in front of the garage apartment and knocked on the landlady's door. When she opened it a cautious inch, Blake said, "I'm Blake Mayfield and this is Amaris Channing. We're trying to find Lyle Dunlap. Has he moved?"

The old woman drew her bristly eyebrows together. 'Not that I know anything about. Ain't he up there?"

"No, ma'am. The lights are out and no one came when we knocked."

She pulled a set of keys off a hook by the door and waddled out. "He better not have run off. He owes me two months' rent."

"We don't know that he moved," Amaris explained hastily. "Maybe he just isn't home."

"I don't know. I heard some funny sounds in the middle of the night last night, but it was too dark out to see anything. I'm a widow woman, and I was scared to go out by myself and see what was going on."

She led them back to the apartment, gave a perfunctory knock and put the key in the lock. She pushed open the door and flipped on the light. "God, what a mess," she lamented. "That's what I get for renting to a bachelor."

The room was indeed in disarray but not what Amaris would have called a mess. She had heard Grace often complain that Lyle wouldn't pick up after himself, and she wasn't surprised to see several days' worth of newspapers scattered about and a few unwashed dishes in the kitchen sink.

Blake examined the closet and bathroom. "No clothes. The medicine cabinet is empty, too. I'm afraid he's gone."

Amaris turned back to the old woman. "Have you seen two young boys over here?"

"No. No, I don't allow no kids in here."

"This is very important. The boys are about this tall," she said, indicating their sizes with her hand, "and they both have brown hair."

"I told you no. He knew better than to come bringing a passel of kids in." The old woman was glaring at the dishes in the sink. "That's what I get for agreeing to rent him a set of dishes. Said he didn't have nothing

it his clothes, and I was fool enough to feel sorry for
m."

Amaris went to Blake and said, "I think we have to
imit Lyle took the boys and left town. Since he took
s own clothes, it doesn't look as though he has any
tention of bringing them back here, either. It's hard
r me to believe he'd do such a thing."

"Has he ever threatened to do this?"

"Not to my knowledge. He tried to get custody dur-
g the divorce proceedings, but he dropped it before
went to court."

"This is a pretty desperate thing for him to do. Do
ou think he'll try to harm them?"

Amaris gingerly picked up a pillow and held it be-
ween her palms as she closed her eyes. With all her
ight, she forced the fear and worry from her mind
id tried to focus on a bright, clear light. Soon she saw
i image of Lyle lying on the pillow, his cheeks un-
naven and dark circles under his eyes. He was think-
ig of the boys and how much he missed them. His
inging for his sons twisted around Amaris's heart and
ie felt his desolation.

Dropping the pillow, she said, "I don't think he
ieans them harm. He just missed them so much. I've
ever felt such a depression before. He was almost
iicidal."

The landlady had gone back to the door and was
laring at them.

"Well? Are you coming or are you going to stand
iere gabbing all night?"

Amaris wanted to snap at the woman's insensitivity,
ut she refrained. She and Blake went out into the cold
ight and down the steps to the car.

202 Follow Your Heart

"When you find him," the old woman bellowe
"you can tell him I plan to press charges! He can't ru
out on the rent and get off scot-free!"

"Yes, ma'am," Blake said. "I'll tell him."

"I'm going to tell the police, too," she yelled aft
them as they got into the car. "He can't get by wi
cheating a poor old widow woman!"

"She's enough to depress anyone," Amaris o
served as they backed away. "She's still yelling at us

"What she said about the police makes sense,
Blake admitted. "I think we're going to have to bri
them into this."

"I dread telling Grace. Knowing how she feels abo
Lyle, there's no telling what she may do."

Grace was still pacing when they got back to h
house, her face lined with worry. Amaris took h
friend's hand and said, "Lyle has moved."

Grace's pale lips barely stirred as she repeated t
words.

"Is this your coat?" Blake said as he took it from t
back of the chair. "Here. Put it on. We need to repo
this to the authorities."

Grace automatically pushed her arms in the sleev
as he held the coat behind her. "The police?"

"It's just a precaution," Amaris said. "Lyle may st
be here in town but at a new address. He may intend
return the boys after a normal visitation period, but
case it's more than that we need to notify the police.

Moving like a loose-jointed robot, Grace went wi
them to the car. As Blake drove them to the police st
tion Grace was silent, her eyes glassy as if she were
shock.

When they were seated before a uniformed officer
one of the back rooms, the policeman said, "You s:

your sons have been kidnapped by your ex-husband?''
At his utterance of the dreaded word "kidnapped,"
Grace's eyes widened and she looked as if she were
about to faint. "Do you have any proof?" the man
asked.

Seeing that Grace couldn't respond, Blake said, "As
I understand it, he wanted custody of the boys at the
time of the divorce and there are hard feelings between the adult parties involved. Miss Channing and I
went to Mr. Dunlap's last-known residence and found
that he, too, is gone."

The policeman looked up at Blake. "And how do
you fit in all this?"

"I'm her attorney," he said, as if it had all been
prearranged. "My name is Blake Mayfield."

The policeman's eyes flickered in recognition of the
name. "I'm Sergeant Mordock." He gestured at a
woman in street clothes who had just entered the room.
"This is Sergeant Wiley."

Amaris had already recognized her friend. "Bridget!
Thank goodness you're on duty tonight."

"Amaris? What on earth brings you down here?"
she asked, then nodded toward Blake and Grace in
greeting.

"This is Blake Mayfield and Grace Dunlap. It appears that Grace's ex-husband may have taken her
sons."

Bridget's smile immediately vanished. "When did
this happen?"

"I'm...not sure," Grace stammered. "I called them
before I left work to tell them I had to go grocery-
shopping and would be a few minutes late getting
home. When they didn't answer the phone, I just assumed they were playing outside. They have permis-

sion to play outside until dark. I was home by seven-thirty and they were gone!'' The color had left Grace's face as she bordered on hysterics.

"Okay, Ms. Dunlap, just try to stay calm. Joe, would you get us all some coffee? I'll fill out the report.'' The policeman gave his chair to Bridget and left the room.

"Now,'' Bridget said in a businesslike manner. "I assume you are the children's legal guardian?''

"Yes. That's right.''

"What are the boys' names, and how old are they?''

"Todd is nine years old and Ben is seven. That's Todd Martin and Benjamin Lyle.''

"And their last name is Dunlap?''

Grace nodded jerkily.

"Can you give me a physical description?'' Bridget asked as her pen moved swiftly over the pages of the form she was filling out.

"Todd is tall.'' Grace held her hand in the air until Bridget could estimate the height in inches. "Ben is this tall. They both have brown hair and brown eyes.''

"Is their hair dark or light brown?''

"Medium.''

Amaris spoke up. "She has folders on both boys, with a recent lock of hair and photos.''

"Great,'' Bridget said with relief. "You have no idea how helpful that will be. Are there also medical and dental records?'' When Grace nodded, Bridget smiled. "Good.''

"They were both in groups we fingerprinted for Kidcheck,'' Amaris added.

"Wonderful. Now I need a description of your ex-husband, Ms. Dunlap.''

Grace's eyes grew cold. "Lyle is five-ten, with medium brown hair and brown eyes. He has a small curved scar on his left cheek and he weighs about 170. He's ... let me think. He's thirty-three years old."

"Occupation?"

"None."

"He was laid off by the highway department," Amaris explained. "We checked his apartment, but he has apparently moved."

"I see." Bridget wrote all that down and said, "Are you reasonably certain he is the one who took the boys? Have you checked the neighborhood and anywhere else they may have gone?"

"Yes, yes, I've looked everywhere."

"Do you have any reason to believe the children could be in any immediate danger from Mr. Dunlap?"

"Danger!" Grace bolted from the chair. "Oh, God! I never thought of that!"

Amaris pressed her back onto the seat. "Try to stay calm, Grace, so we can finish here as quickly as possible." To Bridget, Amaris replied, "I have no reason to believe he would harm them. I know Lyle quite well, and he loves those boys. The problem is a dispute over visitation and late child support. Grace has denied Lyle all but very limited access to the boys and there have been a lot of angry words between them."

"I see." Bridget added this information to the report. "Once we get the boys back, this will have to be resolved to prevent further problems. Do you understand me, Ms. Dunlap?"

Grace nodded numbly.

"I assume there was no sign of a struggle or any indication the boys were forced to leave their house?"

Again Grace shook her head.

"Okay. That's encouraging. I gather there was no note?"

"None. I looked everywhere. Their clothes are gone, as well as a lot of their toys."

"So we can assume Mr. Dunlap has more in mind than a weekend visitation," Bridget surmised. "Is there anyone Mr. Dunlap is close to? A friend or relative, perhaps?"

"Not unless you count Tiffany McNee," Grace bitterly ground out.

"Flo McNee's daughter?"

Amaris interrupted. "I don't think Tiffany and Lyle are still seeing each other."

"Just the same, we'll check it out. Anyone else? Parents, maybe?"

"Lyle hasn't spoken to his parents in years. I don't even know where they live now. His only brother is stationed in Germany with the air force. I don't have any idea where he could have taken them."

"Do either of the boys have a physical reason to need routine or periodic medical care?"

"No, they're both healthy."

"What about Mr. Dunlap?"

"As far as I know he is, too."

Bridget put the papers into a clipboard folder and shut it. "Let's go to the house, Ms. Dunlap and get the files on your sons. I need to look around for myself."

Chapter Twelve

"Grace, you've got to get hold of yourself," Amaris said as dawn pearled the sky outside the windows. It had been less than twelve hours since Grace had discovered her children had been taken by their father, but it seemed like days. Blake and Amaris had not left Grace's side, and none of them had slept. "You're making yourself sick."

Grace paced to the front door and back as she finished yet another cup of coffee. "I don't care if I'm sick or not. I just want my boys back."

Blake said, "This won't make matters move any faster. Maybe we should call the doctor and get a sedative for you."

"No way," Grace replied. "I have to be able to go get them the minute the police find them."

Amaris sighed as she rose from the kitchen table to go make more coffee for the others. Without the stimulation of caffeine, she felt as if she were asleep on her feet. From the kitchen she called out, "Bridget can't get the report to the district attorney any earlier than eight-thirty this morning. So far the police are only patrolling here in town."

Grace groaned. "I'm so worried about them! Do you suppose they had a warm place to sleep last night?"

Blake went to her and put his arm around her as if they had been friends for years. During the long night's shared vigil, a comradeship had developed between them. "I'm sure they were fine. Lyle must have had some plan before he took them. They're probably at one of his friends' houses or in a motel."

"Lyle hasn't got money for a motel." Grace's face was haggard from lack of sleep and worry. "Where could they be?"

Amaris plugged in a fresh pot of coffee and went back into the living room. "I'm going to go back up to their room and try psychometry again."

Grace turned to go with her, but Amaris shook her head. "Let me try it alone."

Upstairs, she closed herself away in the small bedroom. For a minute she simply stood there willing herself to relax, mentally centering her thoughts on the task at hand so she could tune into the surroundings. Slowly she drew in several deep breaths, then began examining the things the boys had left behind—an old tennis shoe, a chocolate bar, the warm earth smell of their active bodies.

Crossing the room, Amaris sat on one of the twin beds. She gathered the pillow against her chest and closed her eyes as she changed her breathing rhythm to the carefully measured cadence she knew would lead her into deeper concentration. At once she felt the hopes and trials and emotions of Todd.

She sent her mind after the tenuous thread that linked him to this room. She knew he was worrying over a math test that he hadn't told Grace he had failed. She saw him trading his second-best pocket knife to Jason in return for an almost-real-gold good-luck charm. She saw an argument with Ben and the midnight snack he had sneaked upstairs from the refrigerator. All were events in the past.

Stilling her mind even further, Amaris tried to see him in the present. For one brief moment she found him and got a glimpse of a second-rate motel room. Her main impression was one of stale hamburger smells and shades of tan and beige and a cheap print on a wall. Then the link was broken and she was almost overwhelmed by Grace's fears.

Amaris drew in a deep, calming breath and concentrated harder. *Think to me, Todd,* she willed. *Let me in.* For a moment she thought she had touched his mind again, but the images capriciously dissipated and once again Grace's panic filled the void Amaris had created for Todd's thoughts.

With a sigh of frustration, Amaris opened her eyes and looked around the room. Grace's thoughts and emotions were so strong they rushed in whenever Amaris relaxed enough to reach Todd. But there was more to it than that, she thought. Todd was deliberately blocking her efforts to contact him with telepathy.

She looked down at the pillow as if it could give her an answer. Grace had been discouraging the boys from practicing their psychic games lately and certainly Lyle forbade it, but Todd had a natural gift. Since Lyle couldn't possibly know his son was using telepathy unless Todd admitted it, Amaris had to conclude that Todd himself was refusing to lead her to them.

There was no point in trying to contact Ben, she decided. He was only seven and although she had been

able to link minds with him before, he might not eve
know the name of the town where Lyle had taken ther
Also she had worked with Todd for two years long
than Ben and he was the stronger telepath of the two

Still carrying the pillow, Amaris went back dow
stairs. "Do you mind if I take Todd's pillow with m
to my house? I'm having trouble concentrating rig
now, and I may have more luck when I'm at home."

"Of course you can. I called my sister Helen
Lynchburg and she's on her way over. I guess I shou
have called her last night, but somehow I thought the
would come home before now."

Blake said, "We'll stay until she gets here."

"There's no need," Grace told him. "It'll take h
an hour and a half or so, and that will give me time
bathe and freshen up." She managed a shaky laug
"Once again I see you in the early hours of the mor
ing, all dressed up, fit to kill. I'm sorry I kept you u
all night."

Blake smiled. He had loosened his tie but still wo
his suit coat. "I'm glad you caught us last night b
fore we left Amaris's house. I only wish we could ha
been more help."

Grace nodded her appreciation, evidently refraini
from speaking for fear the words would bring on mo
tears. She hugged Amaris and stroked Todd's pillow
if she were longing to know whatever it might lat
show Amaris.

"Try to get some rest," Amaris advised. "Bridg
said she would personally take the missing person's r
port to the Franklin County D.A. before she go
home. She's very conscientious and will do all she ca
to find them quickly."

"I know she will. I'll lie down for a while before Helen gets here. I can wait to bathe until then so she can answer the phone for me."

As they drove back to her house Amaris dropped the facade of strength she'd been maintaining for Grace's benefit. "I'm exhausted. I don't know how Grace is holding herself together."

"I know," Blake agreed. "Having your children kidnapped must be a parent's greatest fear."

"At least she had a complete file to give Bridget and their fingerprints are registered with Kidcheck. I've worked with them for years teaching them how to contact me telepathically."

"Then why weren't you able to reach them?"

"It's not that easy. Telepathy is inexact at best. Even the strongest signals can be easily overshadowed by the logical mind. Besides that, Todd is blocking me."

"He's what?"

"I didn't want Grace to know, but he's preventing me from finding them. I saw a glimpse of a seedy motel, but only briefly. I think Todd became aware of what I was doing and blocked his thoughts."

"Can he do that?"

She shrugged. "All he has to do is think about something else. Like I said, telepathy is nebulous. He may not be blocking me consciously. To him it may just seem as if I came to his mind for no reason. Or he may be doing it on purpose."

"Why would he do such a thing?"

"He doesn't want to be found." She ran her fingers through her hair, pushing it back from her face. "You don't know what it's been like for them since the divorce. Divorces are hard on all the people involved, but this has been particularly tough on Todd because he adores his father. They've always been unusually close, whereas Ben is more Grace's child. When Grace suddenly refused to let Lyle see the boys, Todd took it hard. She's been having trouble with him talking back and doing things without permission. He was even caught shoplifting some packages of gum at the grocery store."

"What did Grace do?"

"She punished him and made him take the gum back. I've tried talking with her, but she has her defenses up and won't listen. You see, Grace loved Lyle, and when he left her for another woman all that emotion flipped from love to hate. Now she thinks Lyle is capable of the lowest motives possible."

"I have to say I agree with her. After all, he kidnapped her children."

"You're forgetting they are also *his* children. In a way Grace did the same thing by not letting him see them. Don't get me wrong—I'm certainly not defending Lyle. Right now I'd like to pinch his head off. But there are two sides to this, and I don't believe this is a case of him taking the boys purely to get revenge on Grace. She may have pushed him too far, and with Lyle losing both his job and Tiffany he may have reacted in a desperate way."

"You look awfully tired. You'd better get some sleep."

"First I'm going to take a hot shower, then I'll sleep. I suggest you go home and do the same. After I'm rested, I'm going to try to slip behind Todd's defense and find out where they are."

"Would you like me to stay with you tonight?"

Since Grace's call the evening before, Amaris hadn't given a thought to her decision to confront Blake with her concerns and serious doubts about marrying him. She felt fragile and frightened over the boys and needed Blake's reassuring strength. But they would likely end the evening making love and not only would that strengthen the bond with Blake that she feared she might have to break, but it would distract her from the even more important task of trying to locate Todd and Ben. She reached out and put her hand on the firm muscles of his thigh. ''Don't get me wrong. I want to be with you, but I'm tired and worried. It would be better if you didn't stay. We both need a few hours' rest.''

Blake kissed her, and when he told her goodbye the love in his voice came through so clearly she was touched and regretted having sent him away. But she had had little choice.

Amaris slept until after noon and had only been awake a short while when Blake returned. He wore jeans and a soft blue pullover sweater, his hair was freshly shampooed and his face clean-shaven. ''I brought lunch,'' he said cheerfully. ''Spenser was concerned and had the cook make a big lunch. I didn't have the heart to disappoint them by not eating it. Sometimes Spenser forgets I'm not a little boy any longer.''

Amaris had decided she would have to set aside her worry about their relationship until the missing boys were found, but seeing Blake again made it all but impossible. She loved him. She wanted him. But whether she could have him for her own seemed doubtful. For the moment, she would have to pretend that the boys were her only concern. Forcing a pleasant expression on her face, she returned Blake's warm smile and proceeded to unpack the lunch of deviled eggs, teriyaki chicken and apple pie. "Your cook must think you have an amazing appetite."

"She's been like a second mother to me and her idea of caring is to feed a person. Her husband weighs well over two hundred pounds. For that matter, she probably does, too."

As they ate, they discussed what to do about the boys. Blake was in favor of hiring a private investigator, but Amaris wanted to give the police a chance first. "A probing detective might alert Lyle that we're looking for him," she argued.

"Unless Lyle's a complete fool, he must know we're looking for him. You can't kidnap two kids and expect no one to search for them."

Amaris shook her head. "He might run farther away. The police know how to handle these things."

"So do private investigators. You've been watching too many television shows."

Their discussion was interrupted by the ringing of the telephone. Amaris answered it. "Grace! Is there any news?"

"I just talked to the D.A.'s office," Grace's voice said. She sounded choked by tears. "They aren't going to do anything."

"What?"

"His secretary said the D.A. has decided this is merely a family dispute, a matter for the domestic relations court judge. He says it's a custody problem and not a real kidnapping."

"He can't do that!" Amaris glared across the room at Blake and said, "The D.A. refuses to consider it kidnapping." To Grace, she said, "I'll call him myself!"

"I already talked to him, and it won't do any good." Grace's voice was bitter. "He doesn't want to be bothered."

"Did he say that?" Amaris demanded.

"No, but that's what he meant. He said he's swamped with other work and the divorce courts would be faster."

"Did Bridget give him the copy of your divorce papers showing that you have custody of the boys?"

"Yes. It made no difference. Helen talked to the police department and the information has been sent to the national crime-information center. But since the D.A. won't take action they say it's not going to be treated as an active felony warrant, and the boys' pictures won't be run in the missing-persons bulletin."

"Damn!" Amaris exclaimed. "What do they think we should do? Sit around and see if Lyle decides to return them eventually?"

"I don't know. I have to find a lawyer and get this into court before any action can be taken."

"You've got a lawyer," Amaris said. "Blake told you he will take care of this."

"I know, but I wasn't sure whether he meant it. With the election coming so soon, I'm afraid he won't have time to help me." Grace paused awkwardly. "Besides, Amaris, I can't afford Blake Mayfield."

Amaris put her hand over the mouthpiece. "Grace wants to know what you charge for something like this."

"Tell her it's on the house," he responded.

"What about your campaign?"

"I'll work it in somehow."

Amaris gave him a grateful smile. "Blake will waive his fee. Now stop crying and get some rest. Tell Helen to take care of everything, and you go get some sleep. Blake and I will handle the rest of it."

After she hung up, Amaris said, "That was very thoughtful of you, not to mention generous. But can you believe the D.A. won't file charges against Lyle?"

Blake frowned. "Unfortunately, it is his option. I've never worked with the man, but it seems foolish of him to pass this back to the domestic-relations court. He obviously doesn't realize how serious this is."

"I never thought he would be so hard-hearted. Why, Bridget and I fingerprinted his own grandchildren just last week for Kidcheck!"

"The problem really is that the law allows him the option. As governor, I might be able to get support for correcting this—if I got the backing of the legislature. In the meantime I'm going to hire a private investigator. I think I'll call Jack Bonner. He lives here in the Roanoke area and I've used him before." As Blake placed a call to the man, Amaris took Todd's pillow with her out onto the deck.

Although the day was cool, the sun had warmed the boards beneath her feet and beamed comfortably on her back and shoulders. She sat cross-legged on a chair cushion and let herself become centered. When she felt her body tempo slow and her thought become crystal clear, she took the pillow into her lap and sent her thoughts winging to Todd.

This time the boy was less wary, and Amaris saw the town as he saw it. He was in a car, heading toward the zoo. She saw the sights as he took them in: a church with marble statues inset in its brick front, a uniquely shaped office building silhouetted against the sky, a weather-stained statue on a public street. Ama

iled as she lost the contact. It had been enough. The
ys were in Richmond.

She hurried back inside and found Blake was still on
e phone. "Tell him we think they've been taken to
chmond."

Blake gave her an appraising look but passed the in-
:mation on to the investigator as she'd suggested.

When he hung up, Blake said, "What did you see?"

"Not much, but enough to recognize they're in
chmond. I've been there before, and I'm sure that's
at I saw." She picked up her purse. "Let's go tell
ace."

As Amaris had expected, Grace didn't know of any-
e in Richmond who would take in Lyle and the two
ys. "I saw what looked like a motel room," she told
ace. "I couldn't get the name or location, but I'm
tty sure it was a motel."

Grace frowned. "I thought he didn't have any
ney. How can he afford a motel?"

"How should I know? The important thing is that
boys are safe. They seemed to be on the way to the
."

"Can't we call the police and have Lyle arrested
re?"

Blake shook his head. "Since the D.A. didn't file a
rrant, he is only taking his children on a legal visi-
ion as far as the police are concerned. And Rich-
nd is much too far away for us to drive there and
pe they would still be at the zoo by the time we got
re. If my airplane wasn't in for service, I'd have
ggested we fly there." When Grace looked as if she
re about to cry again, Blake added, "But I have an
estigator, a man named Jack Bonner, who is al-

ready on his way to Richmond. He may contact you directly to get more details.''

Grace nodded. Her sister Helen, who looked like an older and blonder version of Grace, put an arm around Grace's shoulders.

''Besides,'' Amaris said gently, ''how could we explain to the police why we think Lyle and the boys are at the zoo? You know how they generally view psychics.''

Grace had to nod. ''It's so damned unfair! You'd think the police would follow up any lead, regardless of how unconventional it might seem.''

''I can see why they don't,'' Helen said. ''They would be chasing all over kingdom come on wild-goose chases.''

Amaris didn't answer. She knew Helen was not only skeptical because of her conservative upbringing, but it had been Helen's attitude regarding the subject that had given Grace such difficulty in accepting her own psychic gifts.

''I guess we had better go,'' Amaris said. ''I only wanted to return Todd's pillow and tell you what had happened.'' She heard Helen's derisive sniff, but knew Grace understood. ''We'll find them. Don't lose hope.''

''I could never do that.'' Grace clasped Amaris' hands. ''Keep working on it.'' To Blake she said, '' can never thank you enough for offering to help me. I can ever do anything for you, just let me know.''

Blake smiled at her, and put his arm around Amaris ''You're our friend. That's repayment enough.''

As Blake and Amaris walked toward his car, Blake said, ''Come back to Eventide with me, at least for tl afternoon. I gave Bonner that number, as well as yours and Grace's. He can contact us just as easily there.''

"I shouldn't. Grace may need me.''

"She has Helen with her. You still look as if you're ready to drop. You need a break for a while.''

She nodded. "You're right. I slept, but I still don't feel rested.''

"Besides, I hate to say it but it may be days before we hear from Bonner.''

"I know. I just don't want to admit it." She looked around her at the small houses of the quiet town. "Okay. Let's go to Eventide. I need to look out over the mountains and see some distance. I feel hemmed in here at times like this. It's as though the mountains are pressing in on me.''

At Eventide Blake gave Spenser instructions to put through any calls and then escorted Amaris out onto the veranda. Amaris settled into a comfortable chair and as she gazed out at the magnificent view she said, "This is so peaceful. I already feel all my ragged edges smoothing out. This view reminds me of the one from my favorite morning place, the spot where we had our first picnic. I must admit, though, this chair is softer than the rocks on that mountainside.''

"If you decide to marry me, you can sit here on this porch every morning from now on.''

She smiled at him and entwined her fingers with his. "It's so tempting. I love you, Blake. But I don't know I can handle the public exposure." She lifted his hand and kissed it, then rubbed her cheek against it. "Privacy isn't just something I want, it's a necessity for me. You seem not to need any at all.''

'I wouldn't say that.''

"I mean, we're not even married and already the privacy invasion has started. You saw my picture in that paper. I've never been so embarrassed. The reporter took everything out of context."

"I know, you know and so does everyone else. No one believes tabloids like that."

"Someone does, or they wouldn't sell. Not only was I mortified, but it may have already damaged your campaign. I couldn't handle it if I thought you'd lose this election because of me."

"That's all nonsense. This campaign has been based solely on the issues. Neither my personal life nor my opponent's has been a factor in this race—nor will they be."

Amaris put her arms about him and held him close. "I hope that's true."

"And once the election is over most of the reporters will focus on other news stories and it won't be as bad as it is now. Who knows? After a term or two as governor, I may decide to retire from politics."

"No you won't! Certainly not for my benefit. The government needs an honest man like you. A man who's more interested in issues than in politics."

"Then what do you want?" he asked as he buried his face in her hair.

"I don't know. That's why I can't give you an answer yet. Please, Blake. I need more time."

"I didn't mean to press you for an answer," he said then shook his head. "That's not really true. I was pressing you, but it's because I love you and I want to convince you to marry me." Blake knew she needed time to weigh everything involved and that his attempts to sway her would be of no avail. But at the same time he was equally stubborn. He would have Amaris Channing for his wife.

That evening after having taken Amaris home, Blake sat alone in his study contemplating the motives behind his political aspirations. He already had money and prestige. What Blake most wanted to do with his life was to help others—to be of genuine service. Being the governor of Virginia was one way to accomplish that, but it wasn't the only way. Before throwing his hat into the political ring he had accepted the possibility that he might not be elected, and if so he could accept that. But having made the commitment, he was determined to give it his all—just as he was willing to do in marrying Amaris Channing.

Chapter Thirteen

The following morning Amaris was at Blake's house eating one of Eventide's decadently delicious breakfasts. She now knew it was pointless for her to try to shelve her concern over whether or not to marry Blake in order to free her mind to work on trying to mentally contact the missing boys, but she was determined to continue her efforts to reach them. It wasn't Blake's fault that she was having difficulty concentrating, it was her own. The night before she had picked up on what she thought were Todd's thoughts but lost them too soon to be sure. She felt terribly frustrated that she was not being of more help in locating them. She missed them both so much. Todd with his new grown up attitude about being the man of the house, and Ben with his rumpled hair and sweet smile and—

Amaris dropped her fork onto her plate with a clatter and sat bolt upright in the chair, her eyes round with surprise.

"Are you all right?" Blake asked, startled by her sudden movement.

She nodded and made a hushing movement with her hand. For three days, she'd struggled to make contact with Todd, trying everything she could think of. No out of the blue, she seemed to be getting something but not from Todd. After a moment's concentration, she laughed with relief. "I had Ben! Just for a minute there I had Ben!"

Blake leaned forward eagerly, motioning to Spenser that his help wouldn't be needed. Amaris positioned herself more comfortably in the chair. "Let me see if I can find him, again."

She slowed her breathing and let her mind and body relax. Ben. She hadn't tried to contact Ben because he was so young. Todd was better at sending and receiving but he was also better at blocking his thoughts. Ben had not yet learned this.

She pictured Ben as she had last seen him, wearing a sweatshirt that was a hand-me-down from Todd and faded jeans. As her mental picture grew clearer, it began to alter subtly. Instead of a sweatshirt Ben was wearing the rugby sweater she had given him and a pair of the newer jeans Grace had set aside for him to wear to school. She knew she had him.

Ben was sitting on a bed in a room surrounded by symbolically drab colors. It meant he wasn't content to be where he was. Amaris felt Todd was in the room, as well as Lyle, but Ben wasn't thinking about them so she couldn't see them. Ben was thinking about the times he had played the "thought" game with him. That was how he had inadvertently contacted her.

Carefully, so as not to lose touch with him, Amaris planted the suggestion that he look out the window. For a few minutes nothing happened and she thought the contact had slipped away. Then sensations began forming in her mind. Her eyes flew open.

Amaris gripped Blake's hand. "They're at a motel with a picture of a pilgrim on it. I think the name is

'Colonial' or something close to it. I saw bright yellow
with a red star and something in the shape of a rainbow—that part is awfully vague. And doughnuts! I
smelled doughnuts like a bakery would cook!''

"You're sure?"

"As sure as I can be. It never occurred to me to try
to contact Ben instead of Todd!"

Blake reached for the phone and the notepad with
the number of the paging service in Richmond the private investigator had given him. Fifteen minutes after
leaving word for Bonner to call him, the phone in
Blake's study rang. "Mr. Bonner? Blake Mayfield. I'm
glad I reached you. We think the boys are still in Richmond." He met Amaris's eyes and she nodded vigorously. "They're at a motel named Colonial or
something similar to that. It has a picture of a pilgrim
on the sign. Right. And it's close to something large
and bright yellow, with a red star on it and something
like a rainbow. There should be a doughnut bakery
nearby. That's right. Never mind where I got my information." Blake listened to the man, then said, "It
may sound like a long shot to you, but I want it im
mediately checked out." After another short ex
change, Blake hung up.

"Blake, I've got to go to Grace and take her t
Richmond right away. I think this is it. The only prob
lem is that my car has been acting up lately and I don'
know if I can trust it from here to Richmond an
back."

"You sound as if you think you're going withou
me."

"But you said you'd be back on the road again t
morrow and that this next week was crucial to t

campaign." The anxiety Amaris was feeling about going to Richmond was evident on her face.

Blake placed his strong hands on her upper arms and looked directly into her eyes. "You need me to be with you and I'll be there for you. Nothing about my schedule can't be changed."

Amaris nodded, too choked up to speak.

"Spenser, take Miss Channing to her home in Chinquapin so she can pack. Then go by Grace Dunlap's house and pick her up. I will have called to tell her we're going to Richmond. I'll see to it that the plane is ready and I'll meet you all at the airport."

Amaris nodded. "I'll call the police station and tell Bridget Wiley where we're going. I told her I'd keep her informed if we have any leads."

"Okay. And Amaris—don't worry." He gave her a reassuring wink.

As Spenser ushered Amaris from the room, she heard Blake calling Jeff. She was glad Blake had chosen to help her and Grace, and she prayed the change in his schedule wouldn't hurt his chances for election. He was a man of courage and great honor, and the Commonwealth of Virginia would be proud of him as their governor. As they sped away toward Chinquapin, Amaris fought hard to repress her tears of joy and hope that the boys would soon be found.

When she reached her house Amaris tossed a few days' worth of belongings into a bag and called to see Grace was packed. Learning that Grace wouldn't be ready for another fifteen minutes or so, Amaris decided to have Spenser take her to the police station so she could talk with Bridget in person.

Spenser parked Blake's limousine in front of the building and as Amaris was about to go inside a man she vaguely recognized from one of Blake's campaign parties hurried up to her.

"You're Amaris Channing—right?"

Amaris nodded as she tried to recall the man's name.

"James Vanbrugh. *Richmond Times.* Okay if I talk to you? Great," he said without waiting for her to reply.

Amaris was confused. She believed the boys to be in Richmond and fear struck her. "Are the boys all right? Nothing has happened to them, has there?"

"Boys?" Now the reporter looked confused. "What boys?"

She drew back. "Why are you here, Mr. Vanbrugh?"

"I just wanted a personal interview, but," he glanced at the police station, "I seem to have hit pay dirt."

"You've hit nothing. Go away." Amaris brushed past him with more determination than she ever would have used in the past. The reporter, however, was now positive he was on the trail of a story and had no intention of losing the scoop. He hurried into the building after her.

"I said go away," Amaris snapped.

"This is a public building. I have every right to be here. Who did you come here to talk to? Have there been more threats on Blake Mayfield's life?"

That stopped Amaris in her tracks. "What threats on his life? What are you talking about?"

Vanbrugh grinned. "Just fishing. So if it's not death threat, why are you at the police station?"

Amaris glared at him and walked away as briskly as she could. She considered going back to the car and leaving, but she was sure he would follow her. Gra-

was already upset enough without having a rude reporter on her doorstep.

She passed the woman who controlled access to the back offices. "I'm here to see Sergeant Wiley." When the woman nodded for her to go on through, Amaris pointed to Vanbrugh. "He's a reporter and I don't want him to follow me."

Rid of Vanbrugh, Amaris hurried back to Bridget's office. The policewoman was sitting at her desk, reading through some files. When she saw Amaris she smiled and gestured toward a chair.

As Amaris sat down she said, "I'm sure the Dunlap boys are in Richmond."

"Richmond? How are you sure? Who contacted you?"

Amaris hesitated. This was the tricky part. "They did. The boys. In a way."

"What do you mean?"

Amaris drew in a deep breath and plunged on. "They did it by telepathy."

"Oh." Bridget straightened and looked at Amaris as if she thought her friend had slipped a few cogs.

"Surely the police here have used psychics from time to time."

"In Chinquapin? You've got to be kidding."

"Well, whether you have or not, I'm sure of what I saw. I recognized a statue, a church and the shape of a building. That came from Todd. Then this morning Ben sent me the picture of the motel. There's the picture of a pilgrim on the sign and the name is something like Colonial. There is something bright yellow with a rainbow and a star. A red star. And I smelled doughnuts. Aren't you going to write this down?"

Bridget gave her a disapproving frown. "I don't think you should joke about something so serious. I mean, this is a kidnapping, not some game."

"Game? I'm not playing a game. I want you to tell the FBI."

"They'd laugh at me. And then if you hit it lucky and they found those kids around a yellow building with what? A rainbow? They might consider you to be an accessory to the crime."

"But that's where they are!" Amaris protested. "I've been psychic all my life, but I've never tried to trace a missing person until now."

"You never mentioned being psychic before," Bridget skeptically observed as she reopened the file she had been reading.

"I know, but I am and I can help."

"Amaris, go home. You're worried about those kids and it's only natural your mind would play tricks on you. I won't tell anyone what has happened here."

Amaris felt numb with frustration. "I don't care who you tell. I came here so you *would* tell someone— the FBI."

"I'm doing you a favor in not telling them. Go get some rest. You look exhausted."

With a sigh Amaris accepted defeat. At least Blake had contacted the private investigator. "Is there a back way out of here?"

Bridget nodded and pointed her down the correct hall. For a minute she watched Amaris walk away. They had known each other for years. Amaris had worked with her in fingerprinting the schoolchildren Bridget knew it wasn't like Amaris to lie about some thing like this and she was too levelheaded to go off on some wild tangent.

She went back to her desk by way of the central office. "Anything for me?" she asked the woman at the desk.

"Miss Channing was looking for you."

"I just talked to her. It was really odd, May Ann. She said those Dunlap boys—the kidnapping case—had contacted her telepathically."

May Ann snorted. "She sounds like a nut case to me."

Bridget didn't correct her, but as she went back to her desk she considered calling the FBI agent to report what Amaris had said. She never noticed James Vanbrugh sitting in a chair and listening to every word they said.

Chapter Fourteen

Blake's private investigator moved fast. By the time Amaris, Grace and Blake reached Richmond, he had located the Colonial Arms Motel, the Red Star Laundry and the Over the Rainbow Bakery, all of which were clustered together in a heavily industrialized neighborhood.

When they went to the Richmond police with the information, Amaris was pleasantly surprised to find them far more receptive than Bridget had been. They were impressed that the images of the buildings and details she had telepathically picked up were quite accurate. A police unit was immediately dispatched to the motel to see if the desk clerk recognized photographs of Lyle and the boys.

While they waited for the police report, Amaris fed Grace endless cups of coffee and Blake paced. Within the hour the police returned to the station with Lyle handcuffed in the back seat and Ben looking scared half out of his wits.

Grace snatched Ben up and hugged him until he squirmed. With tears streaming down her face, Grace lunged at Lyle. A policeman kept her from physically attacking him. "Where's Todd?" she screamed. "What have you done with him?"

"I...he went to the soft-drink machine to get a drink. I guess he saw the police handcuffing me and heard Ben screaming and he ran away."

"Ran away! My Todd is out there alone? You just left him there?"

Lyle shifted in the chair and the two policemen watched him warily. "I tried to get the policeman to let me stay and help find Todd, but they wouldn't listen to me."

"Two more cars have been dispatched to the neighborhood," one of the policemen said. "They'll find the boy."

Amaris put one arm around Grace's shoulder and smoothed Ben's hair. "Are you searching all around the motel?"

"Yes, ma'am," one of the policemen said. "And we're gradually extending the area we're searching. If he sticks his head out we'll find him."

Grace turned to Lyle. "This is all your fault! If Todd turns up dead, it'll be your fault!"

Lyle's face was as ashen, as if Todd had already died. "My fault! Who pushed me to this? Who denied me the right to see my own kids!"

"Arguing won't solve anything," Blake interrupted. "Both of you were in the wrong, but Lyle, you committed a serious offense. Kidnapping is a federal crime."

Lyle hung his head. "I know," he said miserably. "Don't you think I know that? I wasn't thinking of it as a crime at the time I did it. I just wanted some time with my sons."

"You can't always have everything you want!" Grace stormed. "I have rights, too!"

"Calm down," Amaris advised. "We need to work this out."

Grace made a visible effort to calm herself. "What did you plan to do with them, Lyle? Maybe that will give us some clue."

Ben raised his head. "We were going to a dude ranch. Todd was going to get his own horse, and I was too."

"A dude ranch!" Grace's tone was scathing. "That's just another of your father's stupid pipe dreams."

"Quit trying to turn Ben against me, Grace." Lyle looked as if he wished she would drop dead on the spot.

"Please," Blake said, "this is getting us nowhere. Now, Lyle, think back. Is there any place Todd spoke about that he may have run to?"

Lyle shook his head. "We went to the zoo and the museum and the planetarium. Places like that, but none of them are within walking distance of the motel. Besides, Todd wouldn't go to the zoo at a time like this."

Blake said, "All we can do is wait to see if a patrol car spots him and brings him in. It will be dark soon. Surely anybody seeing a boy out alone at night will report it."

One of the policemen shook his head. "Not necessarily. Some parents let their kids wander around at all hours of the night, and folks don't want to get involved. But we have two extra patrol cars in that area and they all have the boy's description. They're our best bet. We're hoping to find him before dark."

Grace shook her head as tears cascaded down her cheeks. "Isn't there something we can do now?"

"If I were you," Blake said, "and as your attorney I strongly recommend it, you and Lyle need to get some professional help—not to patch up your marriage, because from the looks of things it's too late for that, but so you two can work out enough of your problems that you don't further confuse your children."

Grace looked at Lyle as if he were a snake. "I don't want to work anything out with him."

"I feel the same way about you," Lyle retorted.

"In that case," Blake replied, "the courts may have to reexamine the issue of custody."

"You mean I may get them?" Lyle exclaimed.

"No, I mean they may need to spend some time in foster homes." Blake was primarily bluffing, but he added, "I've known a few cases where custody with neither parent was deemed to be in the child's best interest."

Grace's eyes widened. "A foster home!"

Lyle glanced at Grace, then looked back at Blake. "I guess I could agree to counseling," he grudgingly agreed.

"I guess I could, too," Grace finally admitted. "But neither of us has enough money to pay for it."

Blake smiled. "There are plenty of good agencies that operate on a sliding scale. Amaris and I will help you find one."

Amaris nodded. "I already know someone I can recommend."

Three hours later Grace sighed as she rose and moved to the window. Outside, the night was sooty black, with only occasional puddles of orange-hued light from the street lamps. "I can't believe Todd is out there alone. The very thought makes me feel sick to my stomach.'' She crossed her arms, hugging herself in an attempt to feel more secure. "Anything could happen to him!"

Amaris went to her. "Don't frighten yourself more than you already are. The police are looking for him and they'll bring him back."

"In the meantime," Blake said, "we need to find a motel and try to get some rest. If there's any news, I know the police will contact us."

The policeman nodded. "When you get settled in, call and leave the number with the dispatcher. We could find him any time now."

Reluctantly Grace allowed Amaris to lead her away as Lyle was taken back to his cell.

As they left the police station, Blake said, "They will hold Lyle overnight. The officer he hit when they tried to question him at the motel has until tomorrow to decide if he wants to press charges. By morning, Lyle may think of some place Todd might have been likely to go."

Grace looked as if she didn't trust any suggestion of Lyle's, but she was smart enough to keep her opinions to herself.

Amaris tried again to link her mind with Todd's, but once again she failed. She was too worried to concentrate and that compounded her feelings of frustration.

No one slept well that night. Amaris shared a room with Grace and Ben since she could tell Grace was frightened to be alone, and they talked until the wee hours before Grace finally fell asleep from sheer exhaustion. As Amaris lay there staring up into the darkness she felt lonely, even though Grace was in the room with her. She wanted Blake. Now that she ha

soothed Grace's fears, she had to deal with her own.
She considered going to his room, but she knew that
would only confuse her more. She had to decide
whether she could live as public a life as Blake was offering and whether she could bear it if she turned down
his proposal. It was a terribly difficult decision.

Reluctantly Amaris forced herself to relax. She
would need all her strength and mental resources for
the coming day. As she drifted off to sleep, she told the
vigilant part of her mind to search for Todd. More than
once, she had resolved a problem in her dreams.

Just before daylight Amaris was jarred awake by a
clanging noise in her mind. While Grace slept, Amaris
dressed and went to Blake's room. She knew she was
connecting with Todd.

By the time she got Blake awakened and moving, it
was already good daylight and Amaris was still waiting for Blake to finish shaving. "Can't you go any faster?" she asked.

"Not and keep my chin. I'm doing the best I can.
Just what are you getting from Todd?"

"I'm not sure. I keep hearing these noises that sort
of echo and sound metallic. Like something metal being tossed onto concrete. Todd isn't sending out a
message to me, but he isn't blocking, either. I feel a
strong need to be out there looking for him."

When Blake's phone rang, Amaris's heart began
racing in anticipation that it was the police notifying
them that Todd had been found and was safe. Blake
quickly answered, but shook his head to Amaris when
he heard the voice on the other end. "No, I haven't
read it. No. I told you last night I have things of greater
importance to attend to. The campaign will have to
wait. My decision is final." Without further word

Blake returned to the sink and sluiced water over his face to rinse away the remnants of shaving cream, then dried his face on a hand towel. "Is Grace ready to go?"

"No. I'm letting her sleep. I left her a note telling her we went for an early drive and for her to stay put until we get back. I didn't want her with us. She means well, but sometimes her thoughts jam my frequency, so to speak." Amaris's eyes searched Blake's face. "Was that Jeff?"

"Yes. He's not too happy with me right now."

"It's all my fault. I'm taking your time when you need to be elsewhere."

Blake leaned down to kiss her as he buttoned his shirt. "Let me worry about that. Let's go."

After pulling on a teal sweater that was almost the same color as his eyes, Blake grabbed his coat, and together they headed for the motel where Lyle and the boys had been staying.

Traffic was light as they were an easy hour ahead of the morning rush hour, and with Amaris's directions from her survey of the map while she waited for him to get ready, they had no trouble finding the address the police had given them.

The motel was rundown and fairly nondescript, and Amaris wasn't at all sure they had the right place until she saw a garish yellow building with the words "Red Star Laundry" printed over a red star. "Look at the other building," she said. "See how the name of the Over the Rainbow Bakery is written in an arch? That must be why I saw only a rainbow instead of word And the motel sign has a pilgrim on it and the name 'Colonial Arms.' That Ben has such a fine talent!"

Blake studied the landmarks she had described. " have to admit he did a good job. No wonder we we able to find them so easily. I just wish the police had found both boys." He gave her hand a squeeze. "Don't worry. We'll find Todd."

"I hope the police don't tell anyone about me using telepathy to find them. As much flack as the Reagans caught over astrology, the press would have a field day if they hear you want to marry someone like me. People can be so narrow-minded."

"Let me worry about my image."

Amaris relaxed and centered herself to try again. She laid her hands palm-up on her thighs and closed her eyes. After a moment she opened them again and said, "I have him. Turn left at the next corner, then left again at the light."

After several more turns they were on a street where metal warehouses butted up side-by-side. "Are you sure about this?" Blake asked as he followed Amaris's instructions and turned down a narrow street between more of the tall warehouse-type buildings.

"It doesn't look right, does it?" she said doubtfully. "This seems too far away from the motel." She sat back on the seat. "I must be mistaken but I keep seeing what appear to be huge black tree trunks."

"Maybe we should go back to the motel and try it again," Blake suggested.

"No. I know this place seems unlikely, but I'm sure we're close. Park over there and let's walk."

The buildings that lined both sides of the narrow street were big and old, with only an alleyway separating one from another. Most appeared to be abandoned. Blake tried one of the doors, but it was locked. "Unless he locked the door behind him, Todd isn't in here."

Amaris paid him no attention for she was trying to keep logic and reasoning at bay. Following her intuition, she continued down the street to where several cars were parked. This building was open, and inside she could see several men working. Drawing a deep breath and visualizing herself in the center of a dome of pure white light, she went in the door. Blake was only a step behind.

A few feet into the interior of this warehouse, Amaris stopped. Several men were bustling about, but none of them seemed to notice Amaris and Blake. Amaris mentally called on her inner guidance to give her verification that this was the right building and almost instantly she heard the clang of a tire iron that had been dropped onto the floor. That sound was the same one that had awakened her. For the first time, she was certain she was right. Ignoring the men, she headed for the pile of tires in the back. "Hey, lady," one of the men called out. "Don't go back there. Can I help you?"

Amaris didn't answer. She felt Todd so near that all her attention was centered on him.

"Lady, I said you can't go back there," the man protested. She heard the words clearly, but they seemed to be coming from a great distance.

She heard Blake draw the man's attention, but knew she'd have little time to find Todd before the man threw them out for trespassing. If she didn't catch up with Todd now, he might run again. She could feel his fear and she tried sending him reassurance, but his anxiety blocked it. As she wound her way through the tires which towered high above her head, she had a fleeting thought that this was like a journey through a surrealistic forest of black trees. At the sound of running fee behind her, she quickened her pace. She was certain of each move she was making and felt Todd closer with each step. Rounding what she hoped would be the last turn she saw the young boy near the back wall, curled up on a pile of rags. "Todd!"

He jerked his head up, and when he recognized her he threw himself into her arms. "Aunt Amaris! I'm so glad you're here! The police arrested Ben and Dad and took them away to prison!"

Amaris held him as his body shook with his sobs. Gently she smoothed his hair. "Ben is safe and with your mom. The police only wanted to ask your dad some questions. It's all over, Todd. Everything is all right now."

At least it was for him. She looked at Blake and tried to tell herself no one would ever know about her psychic abilities and that dating her couldn't damage his political career.

WHEN THEY RETURNED to Eventide Jeff was waiting for them. As soon as they got out of the car he shoved a newspaper at Blake. "Read this!"

Amaris leaned closer to Blake to read, "Mayfield Lover is Psychic." Below it was the earlier picture of her tripping down the steps, but now it was cropped to show a close-up of her face. Her mouth was open, her eyes wide and she looked as if she might be screaming some gibberish. "Damn!" she whispered.

"It's not your most flattering picture," Blake said as if he were amused.

"How can you be so calm about this?" she demanded. "What will this do to your image?"

"I can tell you what it will do," Jeff snapped. "It will destroy it! And it's all your fault."

Amaris glared at Jeff, but before she could say what she was forming in her mind, Blake said, "Back off, Jeff. You're out of line."

"Me? Out of line? Think again. This paper is plastered in every news rack in town. Read it!"

Amaris and Blake read silently and Amaris groaned softly. Most of the facts were inaccurate but they were presented in such a way that the average reader would believe them. It also stated that Blake had canceled a speaking engagement to go to Richmond with her. "Blake, no! I told you not to cancel anything."

Blake gave the paper back to Jeff. "It's a small paper and not widely distributed. I'm not worried about it."

"Well you sure as hell should be," Jeff roared. "I was afraid of something like this. My phone has been ringing off the hook all morning. You don't know how hard I've worked to present exactly the right image to the public. A slip like this could cost you the election!"

Amaris began to back toward the car. Jeff was right. If Blake lost the election, it could be all her fault. "I'll call the paper," she said in a pained voice. "I'll tell them it was all a mistake and that Blake and I have broken up."

Blake frowned at her. "You'll do no such thing. Damn it, this is being blown all out of proportion. So you have a talent that happens to be unusual—so what? It's something to be proud of. If you hadn't been able to do what you do, those boys might not have been found for several weeks. Maybe never!"

She could only press her face into her hands and shake her head. "I'm too confused," she said. "I'r not used to having someone record and examine my every move. I can't live in a goldfish bowl. I can't!"

Blake moved toward her but she backed away. "Just take me home," she told him. "I have to think."

He did as she asked and the silence hung tight between them.

"EVERYONE HAS BEEN so helpful and understanding about all this," Grace said as she poured Amaris another cup of tea. "I just got off the phone with Frank, and he told me not to worry about a thing. Judy Abbott is going to fill in for me so I can go to counseling once a week. And I was amazed that the counseling center managed to get us in so quickly. I thought it would be weeks before we could see someone. It's been only two days."

"That really was quick. Bridget said she thought she might be able to pull a few strings, considering all that had happened. How did your first session go?"

"Okay, I guess. Lyle and I aired some grievances that we'd never talked about before. He says I never had time for him, and that's why he let Tiffany into his life. I still don't agree with what he did, but before I didn't know he had a reason at all."

"How do you feel about the boys going to visit him this weekend?"

"I still don't like it, but I guess I have to do it. Yesterday he called about a job application he'd put in with a company in Rocky Mount several weeks ago, and they told him they'd been trying to reach him for a follow-up interview. He says if they hire him, he's moving there so he'll be close to work."

"That would mean the boys would have to go to Rocky Mount for visitation."

"I know, but it's only a few miles, and if Lyle has a job he can help support them again. That will be a big load off my mind."

Amaris smiled at her friend. "You seem more like your old self already." She wished her own problems were resolved. Blake had left town on business immediately on their return from Richmond, but he was back by now and would soon call her. She had stopped at Grace's house in the hope of gathering courage, but nothing helped. She had to tell him it was over between them, and she had to do it face-to-face. Her heart was breaking, but it had to be done.

HALF AN HOUR later, Spenser showed her into the morning room where Blake was reading the newspaper. Light from the expansive windows splashed over and around him like a nimbus, and Amaris wondered how she could bear not to have him in her life. He was so loving and handsome—everything she had ever wanted in a man. If only she herself were different. For a moment she considered renouncing all she was and all she believed in. But that wouldn't change her past, and that alone would be enough to ruin him politically.

"I have to talk to you," she matter-of-factly said as Blake rose with a welcoming smile. Her face was stiff from suppressed emotion.

Sensing her concern, he asked, "It's not the boy again is it?"

"No." She went to the window and gazed sightlessly at the paddock where three sleek red horses were grazing. "It all started here in this room. This was the first place we spoke. Remember?"

"Yes, I do." He was still standing there, staring warily at her. "Amaris, there's something I have to tell you. I've—"

Amaris interrupted him, unable to hold back any longer, "Blake, I can't see you any more." In the ensuing silence, she was sure he, too, could hear her heart break.

"What?" he said at last.

"Don't try to talk me out of it. I have to say this. I'm calling it all off."

"Why?" His voice sounded deep and dangerous. Amaris didn't dare turn to face him.

"Because of what I am. I can't put my psychic ability aside. It's who I am. I really wish I could, but it's impossible. Bridget has asked me to work with the police in Chinquapin, and yesterday the Roanoke police called me about a case. They seem to think I can help them and I said I would. In a lot of people's eyes this would make me seem too liberal, if not downright crazy, but I feel I have to do this if I can. You don't need publicity like this at this point in your career. I've asked that my work be kept secret, but I can't guarantee that word won't leak out."

"You haven't said how you feel. Does this mean you no longer love me?"

Amaris turned, her eyes brimming with tears. "Not love you? I could sooner stop my heart from beating than I could stop loving you."

"Then don't do this to us. Amaris, I love you. If I had met you before I won my party's nomination as a candidate for governor, I wouldn't have stayed in the running. But it didn't happen that way. I've promised thousands of people that I would be the best damned governor Virginia has ever seen, if they would support my election. And by my asking you to marry me, I've promised you that I'll be the best damned husband you could ever hope to find—if only you'll accept. And I always keep my promises. I love you more than any cause or any campaign or any office, and if you marry me and I win the election I'll have to work hard to balance my time, but my highest priority will always be to you and our family."

Slowly Amaris came to him. "I love you, Blake. You're more stubborn than any man I've ever known, but I love you."

"That doesn't answer my question. Will you marry me?"

Warmth spread through her and she felt misty as she nodded. "Yes, I'll marry you."

He smiled as he took her into his arms. As he held her firmly he said, "You may as well learn now that it does no good to argue with a lawyer."

"I didn't promise we wouldn't argue—only that I will marry you." She rubbed her cheek against his chest and breathed in his scent of soap and cologne. "Just remember I warned you."

He held her as if he never wanted to let her go.

THE NEXT FEW WEEKS blurred into a confusing jumble of lunches and speeches and fund-raisers. After the publicity about how Amaris found Todd and Ben in Richmond, she was asked almost as many questions as was Blake. To her relief most of the reporters treated her psychic ability with a degree of respect if not approval and the new cases she was working on remained secret. She began to see evidence that the use of her unusual talent might not hold Blake back after all. Even his opponent's publicists weren't too unkind since she had, after all, located the boys and returned them to their mother.

"I think we should set a date for the wedding," Blake said as they sat before the fire in her living room. "This is the first night we've had to ourselves in weeks."

"I know. I'm exhausted. How about a spring wedding? The mountains are so pretty then."

"Perfect. How does early May sound?"

"Wonderful, but will the new governor be able to take a few days off for a honeymoon then?"

"The state will have to work its schedule around ours. What date is the first Saturday in May?" He reached for his checkbook and opened it to the calendar. "That looks good to me."

"The first Saturday it is, then." She looked at the darkened windows. "It's still snowing. By now the roads will be a mess."

Blake smiled. "I guess I'll have to spend the night. By morning the plows will have it cleared."

"You know what Jeff would say about you staying here all night." She kissed the warm curve where his neck met his shoulder.

"To hell with what Jeff thinks." He gathered her closer in his arms and they made love until the fire flickered out and cold sent them to the warmth of Amaris's bed. There they made love again and fell asleep as dawn paled the sky.

I'M SO NERVOUS I could crawl out of my skin," Amaris murmured. They were in one of Richmond's exclusive hotels in the suite of rooms over Blake's campaign headquarters.

"Relax," Blake said with a smile. "It's all over now but the counting." He took a cup of coffee and one of tea from one of his supporters and handed the tea to Amaris. Only those closest to him and most important to his campaign were in the suite. All the others were crowded in the banquet room below where a large-screen TV was set up to show the voting results.

Amaris looked at him with admiration. She knew he was tired because she was exhausted. They had been on the road almost constantly since she had agreed to marry him. However he looked as calm and relaxed as if they were alone and watching TV after an ordinary date. The other men and women in the room and the one adjoining it were in constant motion, pacing and drinking coffee and eating from the tray of finger foods sent up by room service. From time to time a man or woman would go across the hall to Jeff's room for a cigarette, then dash back as if news might change in the time it took to cross the corridor.

"You really aren't worried, are you," she marveled. "How can you be so collected when I'm a nervous wreck?"

He took her hand and smiled. In a voice that couldn't be overheard by the others he said, "I'm no worried because I know I gave it my best shot. You an I have traveled all over the state and we've talked wit and shaken the hands of everyone we could find. No it's up to the people to make their decision. My bein nervous wouldn't change the outcome."

"True, but it seems to me . . ."

"The fact is, I won't be crushed if I don't win th election. Beating an incumbent governor is a diffic job. I don't agree with much of his political philos phy, but he is an honorable man and he has waged a fair campaign.''

"You amaze me."

"I enjoy being a lawyer—I already know that. I've never been a governor before, so I don't know if I would like that as well. There are changes I want to see in our state government—that's why I ran in the first place. But I'm an influential man and there are other ways of affecting changes.''

The TV program was interrupted for an update on the ballot returns. Blake had a healthy lead over the incumbent. Everyone in the room cheered.

"You're sure to win," Amaris said with barely contained excitement. "You're blowing him out of the water!"

Blake only smiled.

The minutes seemed to crawl by, and hours later as t neared the final tally the governor began narrowing Blake's lead. Tempers became more edgy in the hotel uite. Blake still sat sipping black coffee and leaning ack on the couch. Amaris had kicked off her heels nd was curled up beside him with her shoulder wedged gainst his. She could feel his calmness, and it helped er not to lose her control as all the other, more franc thoughts from the others crowded into her mind. he was thankful Blake was oblivious to them and ished she could successfully block them as well.

The hands of the clock on the end table gradually awled around its face. Twice Amaris got up to check time against that of the digital clock in the bedom, as if the hour mattered. The election would be n when all the votes were counted, whenever that ght be. She found herself pacing and growing more vous, so she went back to sit beside Blake.

She honestly didn't know how she felt. On one hand she desperately wanted Blake to be governor. On the other she didn't think she could stand another luncheon, another rally, another speech, and if he won this race there would be others. She wondered if that was what Blake was feeling, but her thoughts were too disordered to pick up what he was experiencing.

As the night grew later the election returns became less optimistic for Blake. No one was cheering now. At last the news they had dreaded was announced. In spite of his early lead, Blake was now behind and the only ballots outstanding were the ones from his opponent's home county and two of the smaller counties. Everyone's eyes turned to Blake.

He put down his coffee cup, picked up the receiver on the phone beside his elbow and punched in a number he had evidently memorized earlier. "Tom? This is Blake. Congratulations on your victory."

Amaris felt her eyes fill with tears. She wasn't the only one. Several people were wiping their eyes or looking away in an effort of self-control. Amaris threaded her fingers through Blake's and noticed his hands were as cold as her own. At last her thought reached his. He wasn't as unaffected by his defeat as he appeared to be. She smiled faintly as her heart went out to him.

When he hung up, Blake stood and looked around the room. "I want to thank all of you. We fought a good fight, as they say, and it's to Tom's credit that he won. I don't want any of you blaming yourselves." He looked down at Amaris who stood close by his side. "I have to go downstairs now."

She nodded. He had to officially announce his concession of the election. "Just wait until the next general ernor's election," she reassured him. "Tom will be the one making the phone call."

Blake smiled. "We'll see."

Jeff and a few of the others followed them to the elevator. The rest couldn't face the TV cameras and reporters downstairs. The doors slid shut and Amaris felt the elevator descending. She also felt Jeff's glare on the back of her neck, but she didn't respond to it. Jeff blamed her for Blake's defeat, but it was enough to know that Blake didn't.

The doors slid silently open and Amaris's fingers reflexively tightened on his. As soon as he was recognized the reporters and cameramen rushed to capture whatever he might say. Blake put his arm protectively around Amaris so they wouldn't be separated in the confusion.

She had never admired Blake so much as she did as he conceded defeat. He spoke of his opponent's fine qualities and credited both his opponent and himself with having conducted an honest and fair campaign that should make all the voters of Virginia proud. After his prepared speech, Blake was asked by reporters whether he would run again, but he merely smiled and gave an evasive answer.

Amaris was glad when they were finally able to slip away and take a taxi back to the airport. "Are you terribly disappointed?" she asked.

"Not terribly. Are you?"

She laughed softly. "More than I expected to be. *Are you going to run again?*"

Blake shrugged. "Let's see how Tom does. How would you feel about it?"

"I'll stand by you. How does that old song go? 'Wherever we go, whatever we do, we're going to go through it together.'"

"Like I told you once before, I enjoy being a lawyer. You love the mountains and aren't as happy when you aren't in them."

"Four years can bring about a lot of changes. Babies, for instance." She looked up at him as the passing streetlights plunged them from light to dark to light again. "We may be busy four years from now."

He put his arm around her. "You're good for me. Some women would think of me as a failure tonight."

She shook her head. "I'm not Darla. You could never be a failure to me. And like you said, Tom has good qualities."

"Jeff owes you an apology."

"Forget it. He was only trying to do what he thought was best."

"Okay. We can name our first son after him," he teased.

"I wouldn't go that far," she said as she punched him in the ribs.

Blake laughed and pulled her closer. "Let's go home. We have a whole life ahead to plan."

Amaris put her arms around him and snuggled into his embrace. Her mind touched his with love as they rode through Richmond's dark streets.

H A R L E Q U I N

A Calendar of Romance

Be a part of American Romance's year-long celebration of love and the holidays of 1992. Celebrate those special times each month with your favorite authors.

Next month, live out a St. Patrick's Day fantasy in

		MARCH				
S	M	T	W	T	F	S
1	2	3	4	5	6	7
8	9	10	11	12	13	14
15	16	17				21
22	23					
29						

#429 FLANNERY'S RAINBOW
by Julie Kistler

ST. PATRICK'S Day

ᴇad all the books in *A Calendar of Romance,* coming to you one ᴇr month, all year, only in American Romance.

my VALENTINE 1992

Celebrate the most romantic day of the year with
MY VALENTINE 1992—a sexy new collection of four
romantic stories written by our famous Temptation
authors:

> GINA WILKINS
> KRISTINE ROLOFSON
> JOANN ROSS
> VICKI LEWIS THOMPSON

My Valentine 1992—an exquisite escape into a romantic
and sensuous world.

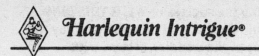

✦ Harlequin Intrigue®

Trust No One...

When you are outwitting a cunning killer, confronting dark secrets or unmasking a devious imposter, it's hard to know whom to trust. Strong arms reach out to embrace you—but are they a safe harbor...or a tiger's den?

When you're on the run, do you dare to fall in love?

For heart-stopping suspense and heart-stirring romance, read Harlequin Intrigue. Two new titles each month.

HARLEQUIN INTRIGUE—where you can expect the unexpected.

Following the success of WITH THIS RING, Harlequin cordially invites you to enjoy the romance of the wedding season with

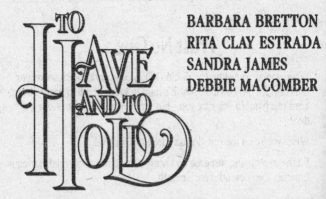

BARBARA BRETTON
RITA CLAY ESTRADA
SANDRA JAMES
DEBBIE MACOMBER

A collection of romantic stories that celebrate the joy, excitement, and mishaps of planning that special day by these four award-winning Harlequin authors.

Available in April at your favorite Harlequin retail outlets.

TH\

Fall in love with

Harlequin Superromance®

Passionate.
Love that strikes like lightning. Drama that will
touch your heart.

Provocative.
As new and exciting as today's headlines.

Poignant.
Stories of men and women like you. People who
affirm the values of loving, caring and
commitment in today's complex world.

At 300 pages, Superromance novels will give you
even more hours of enjoyment.

Look for four new titles every month.

Harlequin Superromance
Books that will make you laugh and cry."

HARLEQUIN
PROUDLY PRESENTS
A DAZZLING NEW CONCEPT IN ROMANCE FICTION

One small town—twelve terrific love stories

Welcome to Tyler, Wisconsin—a town full of people
you'll enjoy getting to know, memorable friends and
unforgettable lovers, and a long-buried secret that
lurks beneath its serene surface....

JOIN US FOR A YEAR IN THE LIFE OF
TYLER

Each book set in Tyler is a self-contained love story;
together, the twelve novels stitch the fabric of a
community.

LOSE YOUR HEART TO TYLER!

The excitement begins in March 1992, with
WHIRLWIND, by Nancy Martin. When lively, brash
Liza Baron arrives home unexpectedly, she moves
into the old family lodge, where the silent and
mysterious Cliff Forrester has been living in seclusion
for years....

WATCH FOR ALL TWELVE BOOKS
OF THE TYLER SERIES
Available wherever Harlequin books are sold

TYLER-G